DISCOVERING WITCHETTY WATERS

By

Trisha J. Kelly

ISBN-13: 978-1544048642
ISBN-10: 1544048645

In memory of my brother.
Egressus autem non sum oblitus.
Gone but not forgotten.

CONTENTS

I would like to thank my family for being my critics! And my friends for their valued support.

CHAPTER ONE

It started off just like every other Saturday really in the Beckett household... Scarlett Beckett perched on the end of her bed deciding exactly what she would be doing today that did not involve having her nose in some book. School days were for books and weekends were for outdoor activity.

Mason Beckett was in the garden shed. He was your typical nine year old lad, well, typical if your stereotype was always up to something. He was concocting a mixture of super strength stink bombs that he was planning to test inside the letter-box of his best friend Charlie's house.

His Hydrogen Sulfide experiment had a putrid smell. He loved science class, it was the only good thing about school.

"Scarlett, can you come down please, and go find Mason we need to talk to you both." Scarlett sighed at the sound of her Mother's voice shouting up the stairs, she had just narrowed down her reading material to a choice of two books, deciding it did look a bit chilly outside.

Please don't say you want me to look after him, again, she thought. There was only so much of Mason that a 13 year old girl could take, such an annoying little brat, and she had not forgiven him yet for taking her iPod apart to see how it worked.

Mr & Mrs Beckett were sitting down at the kitchen table with mugs of steaming hot tea, a letter and other papers. They had stopped talking when Scarlett walked into the room. Grace Beckett was 38 years old and had worked part-time since her children were born. She had a very mundane job really, house cleaning for a few hours a week to help out.

Tom Beckett was 39 years old and he worked in a local Garage where he had been since he left school. He loved tinkering with old cars too in his spare time. Everyone in this family had their own little corners of the world with very different interests and hobbies taking up their time.

Tom Beckett looked very thoughtful and quieter than usual, Scarlett thought. "Did you bring Mason down with you?" he asked.

"Well, he wasn't in his room when I just looked," replied Scarlett. Her Dad got up and walked towards the back door, he could probably guess where his Son had crept out to, either in the garden shed or into the garage.

Tom smiled, his Son was just like Tom was at that age, into everything and probably up to no good! They shared the passion for tinkering with stuff.

"Looks like I got here just in time young man,"

Tom said as he walked into the shed which absolutely reeked of rotten eggs. "Just what were you planning to do with that may I ask?"

Mason knew better than to try and play innocent with his Dad so just grinned at him. "Well it's like this Dad, Charlie Watts punctured my bike the other day, so…" As they wandered into the house Tom was not really listening, he had something very important he needed to tell his children. Problem was, where to begin?

Tom had worked at Percy's garage since he left school, the old man had taught him everything he knew, and now Percy Tatterhill was retiring. Tom had the choice to relocate or be out of work.

He repeated the conversation to them that he had previously with Percy.

"We are going where?" Scarlett could not believe what her Father was telling them. "Run that by me again, I think I misheard you."

"Sounds way cool to me," Mason piped up. It all sounded like a lot of mischief to be had.

Grace smiled, she was secretly very excited about the prospects of what they were doing. She really needed a change from the past 12 years of drudgery, cleaning, cleaning, cleaning! Anything would be better than that.

"Waters End Village," Tom explained again, "that's where we will be moving to. A small remote village that is part of a group of seven islands situated off of the Kentish Coast, which are together known from old folklore as 'Witchetty Waters'."

Mason had his ears on full alert now. Witches hmmm, and much water? This sounded even better by the minute.

Tom picked up the letter and papers on the table. "You like a good read Scarlett, I will let you have a look over it all. I think you will find it interesting. it will tell you a lot more about the history of the place and about the other smaller islands.

"We will be living at No.1 Waters End Village, it needs a lot of doing up and there are many jobs to do on the whole island to bring it up to date and drag it into the 21st century!" Mr Beckett explained.

"Don't worry we will have use of a boat to get to the mainland for supplies and from what I've been told it's quite civilised," he smiled.

Tom was now genuinely excited about his new venture. Mason was deep in thought as to how exactly he could set up a radar and contact extra terrestrials. Grace pondered over her new role in helping with all this.

Scarlett had left the room with all the papers, she now had something different to read over this morning, a third option to while away the hours.

Waters End village being remote was an understatement, Scarlett thought. It looked like an uninhabited expanse of grass and woodland on the online images. with just a few buildings dotted around.

From what she could make out, No.1 was a large dilapidated house with outbuildings, a barn and a garage as far as she could tell… with rotten rooftops.

Intrigued, Scarlett wondered how the name Witchetty Waters fitted into the islands, a nagging thought told her maybe they would eventually find out.

The next two weeks passed by very quickly and now there was a big removal van sitting out the front of the house. Scarlett watched from her bedroom window as the two men were carrying out furniture and loading it up.

She looked around at the bare walls and boxes, boxes which she had very carefully marked as 'fragile'. Everything she owned was precious and fragile to her and should be treated as such.

Very much a loner, she would not be leaving any real friends behind. She had always been a very studious girl often lost in fantasy worlds of all the books she read, far more exciting than boy bands, hair extensions and fake tans. As long as she could remain in touch with the outside world when she needed to then she guessed it may not be all that bad.

Depending of course on who and what was on the islands.

Mason had a lot of dodgy looking boxes that were marked 'Top secret' and 'Keep out' with gruesome stickers, smeared fake blood and threats of tarantula bites for added scary effect.

He had thought that they had overlooked the fact there would be no school on the island, no school meant no more teachers. Well as it turned out he would be wrong about that.

By lunch-time the family said goodbye to their house in Norfolk and set off behind the removal van on the journey down South. As it would turn out, this journey would be very much further than from A to B, much further in fact.

The islands had been in Percy Tatterhill's family since the 1400s, during the reign of Richard 11 who took claim to them. One was originally used to place storage buildings and had many concealed tunnels which contained all forms of contraband.

Pirating was rife and the King staked his claim against the smugglers. It was his right, his pieces of eight.

In return for overseeing and guarding many treasures, the Taterhill family were the keepers of the islands and indeed inherited everything there was to gain long after the demise of the King.

As the centuries passed only one island was in use. It had been the home to Fishermen, Farmers, Doctors and Teachers, the very basics needed in small communities... *but* not all inhabitants were invited.

It did not take long for Mason to become irritating in the back of the car. Scarlett zoned out once again trying very hard to concentrate on the line she had just reread four times. Hopefully he would find many places to get lost in for a very long time at Waters End.

Miss Vickery stoked the fire and threw on another couple of logs, the small flames crackled back to life and one very content large black cat stretched out his long legs to their full extent and flopped back on his side.

Spangles was very content and in no particular hurry to venture anywhere just for a while.

Elvira Vickery was a 62 year old spinster and she was the occupant of No.5 Waters End. Her only company was Mr Spangles, her 14 year old tom cat, it was all she needed.

A cat he may be but not just any old moggy, oh no, he was special, very special and in fact descended from a long line of very able felines that had dwelt for many years on the islands.

Miss Vickery was going to be a private tutor. She had received a letter two weeks ago from Mr Percy Tatterhill... Scarlett and Mason Beckett aged thirteen and nine, perfect.

It was late Autumn and by the time the Becketts arrived at the boatyard awaiting the ferry it was already turning into a dusky sky and there was a nippy chill in the air. Scarlett was busy taking in her surroundings, and standing alongside the boats that were jangling in the breeze she noted that the islands were not in view from the mainland.

Her parents were busy chatting away and oblivious to the fact that Mason was shaking up a bottle of Coke and spraying it all over a small fishing boat. "I name this ship the..." he did not get any further before Scarlett grabbed the bottle and yanked him away by his collar.

A little while later they were making their way across the English Channel on the twenty minute journey to Witchetty Waters. Not too far thought Scarlett, after all she would want to come back and forth a couple of times a week, at least.

As the ferry approached the islands, many pairs of eyes were upon it and one man was watching through his binoculars.

Septimus Dread was every bit and more the stuff that nightmares were made of. Standing at over six feet tall with grey straggly hair and an unkempt beard he crept through the edge of the forest with a scowl on his rugged face muttering into the night air, "Looks like we have company." The dark ravens squawked overhead in reply to his mutterings.

"Do you think there will be food waiting for us Sis? I'm really starving." Mason's tummy rumbled loudly to agree with him.

"Yep, wild berries and a raw fish be the best you can hope for tonight," came the sarcastic reply. It had been a long day.

Percy Tatterhill had been relaxing nicely in his Georgian Townhouse indulging himself in a glass of the finest malt whisky from his personal cellar. A gentle burn worked down his throat as he took a large gulp of his favourite tipple.

He settled down with a fine Havana cigar which he set aside in his large crystal ashtray. This was the life, he thought. He had finally closed down his garage and now he could put his feet up and have a well deserved rest.

Strolling over to the fourth floor window, he perched himself next to his telescope and swung it around zooming in on the late afternoon ferry which was now a very small shape in the distance. If anyone deserved to take over the deeds to the islands it would be Tom Beckett and his family.

Of course there was a lot of hard work involved, Percy knew this and was only too aware of what was at stake.

Percy had never married, he almost did once but that was not to be, circumstances seemed to always get in the way. Instead he had focused on the business he built up, and enjoyed many hours working on the cars and teaching Tom all he knew. The boy had done well and took to it like a duck to water.

The islands were left to take care of themselves over the years with carefully placed residents in the houses that were directly employed by Percy Tatterhill.

Now the time had come to hand over the reins, but more importantly it had always nagged away at Percy that so many wrongs committed over many years now needed to be put right. He hoped that he had chosen wisely and that the Beckett family were now ready (unbeknown to them of course) to start unlocking the ancient keys of the waters, and more importantly to lift the curse.

When he said Beckett family, he meant the Beckett children. All hopes for the future were pinned on them, what could possibly go wrong? He frowned.

Scarlett awoke and for a moment had to focus on where she was. It was very quiet and still dark, then she remembered that they had put mattresses down on the floor and crashed out about ten o'clock the night before.

She pulled the duvet to one side and stood up, shuffling towards the window being careful not to bang into stuff and wake everybody else up. The curtains were dark, old, dusty and smelly. She pulled one to the side and squinted at her watch, tilting it towards the semi light outside. It was just past five o'clock in the morning.

She opened the other curtain and peered out to get her bearings. From her viewpoint at the back of the house there was a low flat roof running from under her bedroom window all along the rear to her brother's bedroom. She made a mental note of the rest of the layout outside.

There was a large expanse of leafy ground and an old barn about 50 yards back, the doors were hanging on loose hinges, she dreaded to think what could be lurking about in there. Several large trees surrounded the edges of the garden space and at the bottom on the right was a very large shed.

From what she remembered, the front of the house had a big double garage to one side, a balcony outside her parent's bedroom, and an old porch surrounding the front door.

There was a very large kitchen with a range cooker and cold slate tiles on the floor, an old scullery with a door leading down to a basement/cellar.

In the living room was a large old inglenook fireplace, and it was a pleasant surprise to find when they arrived that a fire had been prepared for them with a stack of logs chopped in a big basket beside the fire.

There was a huge wooden table in the kitchen and when they arrived they found cooked meats, fresh baked bread, a large pot of soup and various bits and pieces with a welcome note left from Percy Tatterhill. It was a very welcoming gesture for a hungry family!

As Scarlett was thinking back to the previous

evening, she thought she noticed a light darting through the trees like a torch. She rubbed her eyes and stared at the opening between the large pines but saw nothing else. May have been a trick of the light, she told herself.

Feeling her way around the walls for the light switch it dawned on her that there was a very cold chill. Probably coming through the old window panes, she thought. Thinking about it, her Father needed to make the roof tiles his first priority, winter was approaching fast.

Septimus Dread was not in the least bit bothered about being seen, far from it, he would make it a mission to be seen and he wanted to spook those kids right out. The sooner they shifted back to wherever they came from the better it would be.

It would not take long to get rid of this lot of town folk, he was sure of that.

Mason was wide awake two hours later and was underneath the tent he had made in the corner of the room, he had his bright torch perched on top of an empty box.

He was munching away on a bowl of sweets he had taken up with him the night before, and was practising knots, in particular, knots that held body weight, knots to support a hammock.

Being a Boy Scout was very useful, almost as good as chemistry lessons, all super heroes and inventors had their uses. He picked hard toffee from his teeth.

Grace Beckett was busying herself in the kitchen and had a large pot of oats warming away nicely on the stove. The house was much larger than she ever imagined and all in all a bit of D.I.Y around the place and a lot of TLC was all that was needed for Tom and herself to turn this very old house into a perfect family home.

She was very much looking forward to meeting the neighbours dotted around the island.

And with that thought she turned towards the hall as somebody was outside clanging the large bell hanging in the porch.

"Good morning," the young man said cheerfully as he stood back from the doorway and gave a big smile to Grace. He was youthful looking, probably in his early 20s, clean shaven, of average height and build and with a shock of medium brown hair sticking out from under his woolly hat.

"I'm Beanie," he explained and proceeded to hand over a large tray of eggs, with an odd bit of straw attached to them. "I keep a few animals on the island, so don't be alarmed if you catch the chickens wandering around, they like to stroll all over the place. Fresh eggs today and I'll have some fresh milk for you a bit later on. Welcome to Waters End Mrs Beckett, do hope you will stay," and with that he was gone.

Mason jumped off the bannister and karate chopped an imaginary opponent. He had a long yellow scarf tied around his head, it did not belong to him, nor did the test tubes hidden deep in his pocket Never too early in the day to start an important mission.

Mr Spangles jumped up onto the water butt then leapt expertly from there onto the porch. He then floated up and stopped just above the roof line before allowing himself to drop gently down and there he entered through a large gap and jumped down into the attic.

Elvira had sent her feline friend out to do a bit of spying so she had a little bit of an idea what the Beckett children were all about before their meeting. Spangles would tell her all about them and uncover little secrets, always handy to know.

Yes, her cat was an all flying all talking mystical little creature. After all every good witch worth her salts had a cauldron for mixing potions, a heavy book for casting spells and a bona fide magic cat.

She set about blowing the dust off a particularly heavy and very ancient book of spells and placed it on a cast iron stand. It stood behind mauve satin curtains that were covered in stars and lined with gold coloured cloth folded thrice times. They were very heavy and embraced the wooden floor.

Eye of Newt and tail of Snake
Swirls of blood I will make
Ancient days truth be told
Let the seeing days unfold
Bitter grass and milk of goat
To the stars I will float
Muddy waters let me see
If what has been will really be.

CHAPTER TWO

Scarlett sat at her desk that she had now acquired It was a beautiful old writing bureau complete with a blotting pad and an inkwell (not that she was going to use that just yet). It had been covered over with a dust sheet and by the look of it had not been used for many a year. Her Father had oiled it and buffed it up, and also the Captain's chair that went with it. The leather was cold to sit on at first, she swivelled on it just for affect.

Spread out in front of her she had the paperwork and had put it into different sections, the first pile of papers was the one she was interested in right now.

No.1 Waters End

This dwelling shall be occupied by the Keeper of the Islands, the house shall be 'tied' to the position which involves maintenance and general upkeep of all buildings. Day to day running and overseeing of all other services to supply the Islands. Salary to be agreed with successful appointee/s.

No.2 Waters End

Unoccupied storage facility.

No.3 Waters End

Game-keeper's house... position currently filled by:-'Beanie', 24 years old, animal lover and great carer. Responsible for cattle chickens and all wildlife, namely birds, hares, owls, deer, foxes, sheep, goats, otters and the timeless horses.

No.4 Waters End

Unoccupied storage facility

No.5 Waters End

Teacher's house... position currently filled by:- Elvira Vickery, 62 years old, a graduate in specialist subjects and general knowledge, lives with cat.

No.6 Waters End

Unoccupied storage facility

No.7 Waters End

The Medic's House... position currently filled by:- Basil Greenleaf, 44 years old, uses alternate therapies and ancient tried & trusted remedies for all ailments.

All of the above have 'tied' houses and arranged salaries.

Other Buildings Facilities & General.

Small Village Stores located by the Harbour.

Proprietors:-

Mr & Mrs Ted and Nancy Bakewell.

Opening Hours :- As and when

Delivery Service :- Nothing specific.

Self-employed and Semi-retired.

Mr Bakewell fishes mostly and Mrs Bakewell sews and knits.

When open they supply freshly baked bread and lovely cakes, fine organic vegetables all home grown by themselves, a regular stock of frozen cuts of meat and fish.

Log Cabin in the woods

A tied house for the Wood Man, currently occupied for many years by Septimus Dread, 58 years old, good with an axe but not with people.

Other outbuildings :-

Barn

Cattle shed

Double garage

Large shed housing agricultural machinery

Smaller sheds etc.

The landscape of the island consisted of open grazing land, trees, a forest, caves, arable land and the harbour...Oh yes and the Hidden Bay?

That was basically the general description of the island with a footnote that the other 6 islands surrounding Waters End Village were not supplied with Electricity or water and were, in effect, out of bounds to all of the Islanders and deemed 'unsafe'.

Nowhere on this island seemed to be restricted in any way or dangerous to the inhabitants, human or animal.

Well, that seemed to pretty much cover the island part. As to the mainland and what was useful there would be something that Scarlett would work out on her trips over by ferry. It came back and forth two times a week, that was a start!

List to self:- Library, Newsagents, Arts & Crafts.

Septimus Dread towered over his workbench, he had just finished painting words on his 'Danger' signs.

"Darn kids going to be nothing but trouble and get in the way where they weren't wanted, soon see about that," he muttered on under his breath.

He looked at his handiwork. "That oughta do it," he let out a low grunt.

He had spent many years looking around the islands as did his Uncle before him, Lumberjack Big Dread. He was even bigger and scarier looking than Septimus himself, with hands like shovels and beady little eyes for seeing just as good in the dark.

No damn ghosts were gonna bother him, no sir

Ghouls or no ghouls he knew there was gold and treasures buried somewhere, the legends in these parts were well known.

The year was 1397 when the Jolly Sea boat sank in a treacherous storm in these parts. Stories of old told how many treasures had been taken from the Island that had been hidden for years and the Curse of the witches caused the sinking of the greedy men and their booty. Part by part it was retrieved from the waters and hidden... only this time much deeper into places that nobody knew of.

This story had been twisted and turned for many centuries, with bits added on. The only people who knew for sure the whereabouts of where this bounty now lays was a load of old sea pirates living in an in-between world, as he called it and some damn old witches... whereabouts not certain, not certain at all.

Septimus was not going to give up. He had spent too many years searching these woods, searching these caves, searching fields. High and low he had searched for what he considered was rightfully his, of course it was.

'Do not enter these here bat caves', 'Danger sinking sand', 'Swamp area', 'Grass snakes', 'Radioactive area', 'Hazardous materials'. He scooped up his danger signs and set off to carefully place them in all areas he wanted keeping private.

You would not know where Septimus had just been because the old wood storing shed was now covered over with leafy camouflage, the wooden door underneath shut tight with the biggest padlock you could imagine, as was the door to the log cabin.

'Private property' signs were at the front and the rear of his woodland retreat. The only prying eyes around here were dark circling ravens.

In the distance loud banging could be heard, post one was up already.

Scaffolding had been put up at the side of the house and Tom agreed that Mason could be his 'helper' while he was up and down seeing to the missing roof tiles, replacing the guttering and a bit of pointing to the chimney. There were safety nets in place around the edges and it was agreed that Mason stayed on the middle level where the flat roof was.

If Tom had been on his own a multi way ladder would have sufficed, this was the child safe option. Mason was in his element, naturally, he was getting paid in kind.

"Dad if you don't need my help right this minute there's stuff I need to put in the shed, can you manage without me?" Mason was itching to get in them tool boxes.

"You can have ten minutes if you like," Tom shouted back down. He knew Mason's attention span was that of a gnat, he also knew ten minutes was an hour in Mason's world.

But he was willing to let his son explore and make the most of his free week, lessons started next week! Peace and quiet for a few hours a day, then Tom could really make headway.

Grace was in some old working clothes, she had plenty of them and wasn't afraid of hard work. Some well earned treats would be on the cards, they could now afford them. A good wage coming in and no expenses.

Elvira had yet to introduce herself to the Becketts, but they were not strangers to her as Mr Spangles had been very stealthy so far, even managing to get himself invited into No.1 once or twice. This time he chose to saunter up the stairs and walk through the door, as your normal house cat would.

Thus far she had learnt a lot about the family, what they were like, their habits, personalities, hobbies and what they were up to, more importantly what the teenage girl and young boy were made of. Very interesting mix of intelligence and imagination, it was looking good for what she had in mind, nothing like being hands on at lesson times.

It was time to pop over, she thought, and introduce herself to Mrs Beckett. A casual drop in with a tin of specially mixed homemade scones.

Grace Beckett heard the loud clanging of the bell in the porch, set aside her mop and bucket and went to answer the door. Scarlett peered over the top of the stairs intrigued to see who their caller was.

Standing in the porch-way was Miss Elvira Vickery in all her witchy glory. Wow, thought Grace, just who do we have here?

"Mrs Beckett?" Elvira asked, knowing full well who she was addressing. "May I introduce myself to you, I'm Miss Vickery, but please do call me Elvira. Private tutor to Scarlett and Mason." She extended her hand to shake that of Grace.

"Please do come in," Grace replied. "I was just about to stop for a cup of tea, there is so much to do here."

"How lovely, and presumptuous on my part I know, but I have made a little something to go with it." She handed Grace the tin of freshly baked scones and entered the hallway.

Scarlett stayed quite still and watched this woman entering the house. She was extremely colourful in her appearance, with jet black hair and a very straight fringe cut across her eyes. She was a little bit on the dumpy side and quite short, no more than 5ft in height. The most striking thing about her was the satin cloak draped about her shoulders.

Without turning around or looking up, Elvira said quite loudly, "Please, do join us Scarlett."

The three of them sat around the long table. This lady had a very dramatically made up face and funnily enough did not look anywhere near her age. She actually looked to be more the same age as Grace Beckett.

"Do help yourselves please, my own speciality and quite unique fruit scones, I'm sure you will enjoy them."

Mother and daughter obliged and straight away obliged again, very nice too. Elvira did not actually join them but they had not noticed, in actual fact, both of them were trying very hard not to break out into a fit of giggles. Not wanting to be rude they contained themselves to very large grins, they had no idea why, and nor did they care.

"Perfect, isn't this nice? I much prefer a casual meeting with parents and pupils, let me tell you a little bit about myself."

"Please do and take your time, we have no plans

for the next few days, I mean this week, I, oh! Scarlett do you know what I mean? Because I have no clue what I mean at all at the moment."

Grace could not help herself and burst out into a fit of laughter. Scarlett was leaning forward holding onto her stomach because she was laughing so much it was hurting her. Whatever the question was she did not know the answer.

Mason came running into the kitchen and slammed the door shut just before three chickens got to it, phew that was close! He opened the top half of the stable door and looked out at the critters that were walking around in circles pecking around on the floor.

Weird looking things he thought, and they were quick. He would have to learn to run faster, or he needed wheels.

"Do come and join us Mason." He turned around, who was this strange woman sat in his kitchen and what was with the grinning Mum and hysterical sister? It wasn't that funny, he was nearly attacked.

"My name is Miss Vickery, your new teacher. Please sit, would you like a scone?" She could not see him putting up any resistance, and she would be right.

"Yum," he said and took another without asking. She smiled at the boy, the boy smiled at her, the boy laughed at her, the boy fell off the chair laughing. It was a very happy kitchen.

A short while later everything settled down a bit and now the ice was broken, Mum, Daughter & Son Beckett all thought that Elvira was great, and why would they not?

The seed had been planted into their minds that from now on everything Elvira suggested they were very open to agreeing with.

Nothing Elvira concocted was a poison or a danger but non the less it was very powerful, and today the little scone mixture had given her the advantage she needed.

Fruits of forest and tickled rib dough
Takes your mind where it needs to go.

Nobody really remembered the new teacher leaving, she just seemed to have left the house. She had however left some forms to be filled out on the table, one for each child.

Normally Scarlett would have been on the ball and attended to hers immediately, right at that moment though, she was just happy to take a little time out. She smiled at her Mum and her Brother, they smiled back.

"Mason… Mason…?" Where was that boy, Tom thought as he descended the ladder to come down and fetch his own materials. Fat lot of good his little helper was.

Basil Greenleaf was out in his greenhouse tending to his peppermint plants. He thought that maybe one or two may be needed later on that day after he had spotted Elvira tipping out the contents of her biscuit tin onto a compost heap. Up to her tricks again he thought. He also tended to his energising beans and vitality peas, and just for good measure the 'special seaweed'.

Mr Spangles lay across the back of the sofa with one paw preening around his ear and over his nose as Elvira returned home.

Purring away he whispered, *"You look happy Elvira, did it all go to plan?"*

"Of course Spangles," she replied, "teaching will be so much easier now, and I'm sure Mrs Beckett will give full permission for any little trips necessary along the way."

And with that she disappeared into the back parlour where she dialled out on the phone to report back to Percy Tatterhill.

Percy fancied a little company later on that evening and he took himself off to the Coach & Horses Inn for a pint or two and a bit of chatter. He almost regretted it as soon as he walked in, there holding court was Patrick Hinger (known locally as Mr Whinger).

"Hello Patrick, how's things?" Percy enquired as he walked to the bar.

"Evening Percy, well actually things aren't that good since you're asking, the weather is rubbish and it's going to get worse so they say, we are in for it next week. Have you seen the sports pages? That team of ours couldn't score a goal if there was no keeper in the goal mouth. The newspapers were late again this morning and there I am waiting since 5.30 this morning. You tell me why I bother running the shop, then look at that woman in the corner would you, taking up two chairs all by herself she is…"

Percy had long since taken a seat at the other end of the bar where he found the delightful owner of the small corner gift shop *'Contessa Alessa'*. "Good evening Mrs Bonetti," Percy said and he removed his cap. This time he was greeted with a big smile.

"Long time no see Mr Tatterhill."

Patrick was still waffling on to anybody within earshot, not really aware that nobody dared make eye contact with him.

The Coach & Horses Inn had stood the test of time and had been a prominent old pub in these parts for many centuries. It was an old 14th century coaching inn back then frequented by sailors, peasants, traders and anyone looking to do a bit of dodgy business. Nowadays it was just a cosy pub.

CHAPTER THREE

So, they had four days left, Thursday through to Sunday, to finish their settling in period before Scarlett and Mason were to start their private tutoring at No. 5 Waters End, home of Elvira Vickery and her cat.

Tom and Grace had suggested, much to the dismay of Scarlett, that maybe the two youngsters could go off for a few hours and make themselves familiar with Waters End Village. She scowled at her Father but remained silent because he had promised her a little treat when they took the mainland ferry on Saturday, she would hold him to that!

Besides which she had to agree that while the upstairs bedrooms were being painted for her and Mason that it would not be a good idea for the super hero to be involved, nope, not good at all.

To show willing she offered to make a small box of sandwiches, snacks and grabbed a couple of cans from the fridge. Shoving them in her small rucksack she called out to her brother, on the third yell he came bounding down the stairs.

"I'm not deaf you know, I heard you the first time." His arms were cradled around several items that he let go of and they spilled all over the kitchen table.

Torch, notepad and pen, another torch, a small pen knife, something gross in a jar, a tin of green string, a magnifying glass, tweezers, gob stoppers, plasters, an eye patch, compass, and last but not least, a stop watch.

Scarlett sighed thinking, Livingstone I presume. A few minutes later the pair set off, both carrying a small rucksack on their backs. They were wearing old trousers, sweaters, body warmers, a woolly hat and groovy thick socks, complete with green wellington boots.

It was just past 9 a.m., Scarlett thought if she could keep her brother out of the way till at least 2 o'clock that afternoon she could wangle a couple of gifts on Saturday, maybe three.

She had no idea how long it would take to go all around the outskirts of the island but she had worked out that maybe they would have time to go halfway and then stop for lunch and maybe head back on a more inland route.

Mason was not so much taking in the scenery as planning his mission. They were now heading in an easterly direction from their house, he made a note.

Up high on a hill in the centre of the island stood the two majestic timeless horses, so named because they seem to have been there forever. They watched from the distance standing very still.

The winter sun shone on the mist of the grassy plain. They made a stunning sight, a smaller dapple grey horse which seemed to shine like silver with the rays of golden sunlight reflecting from her and a larger very majestic horse of sleek black.

Beanie did not look after these horses, they came and they went. In his mind he took fancy that the small female should be called Celeste, because she was heavenly, a bright light shone about her. The male companion that towered over her he called Apollo, a strong looking stallion. No finer horses had he ever seen.

They did not start their trek at the very water's edge, instead they walked behind the houses that were all spaced out as Scarlett recalled from an aerial view roughly around the Southern part of the island. At least the odd numbered ones were, those marked uninhabited/storage were set right back almost amongst the forest's opening.

Mason also had two deep pockets on the knees of his trousers. He fished into them, a crab line in one and the other had two top end walkie talkies. Him and Charlie had tested them out, came in very handy when they had been on their chemical 'borrowing' mission in the science lab.

It wasn't really stealing because he had planned on putting the apparatus back in the cupboard, but then they moved and he had forgot, so it wasn't his fault, it was his Dad's.

He chuckled because Charlie lost the coin toss, he had to go into the empty classroom, Mason was perched around the corner on 'lookout'. "Over and out, mission compete," Charlie had whispered into his walkie talkie. "I'm outta here."

Maybe in the next School Holidays his buddy would be able to come over and stay. He would love it here, it's so way cool!

"Hurry up Mason we don't have all day." Big sisters, yuck, who needed them? Girls don't have any clue about anything. He stuck his tongue out behind her back and crossed his eyes.

The nearest building to their house was actually the little village store which was situated quite close to the small harbour where the ferry service ran back and forth every Saturday and every Wednesday. One morning crossing and one in the afternoon.

There was also use of a small boat or two that were moored up at the jetty. Mostly there was just one because Mr Bakewell was often out in the other, fishing rod dangling into the shallow waters.

Hardly suitable for crossing from Islands to mainland though, their Dad was a bit misinformed there. Island to island maybe, they just had oars in the smaller boat and a little outboard motor on the larger of the two, with a small rudder.

The Bakewell Store was quite a small affair, a log cabin style with a front porch that had a wooden bench and a row of large coloured outdoor bulbs draped underneath the guttering. There were checked gingham curtains at the front and side windows and large double doors opening out to a back area.

This was where Mr Bakewell had a garden and a greenhouse that was well stocked with potatoes, onions, cabbages and carrots, peas, marrows, swede, turnips and parsnips, lettuces, runner beans, tomato plants and cucumbers.

Apple trees, and plum trees, a gooseberry bush, rhubarb, blackcurrants and strawberries all adorned this wonderful garden, so there was always a supply of seasonal fruit and veg and a cold storage for the winter.

Mason had his binoculars over his eyes and was busy adjusting them. He could see the large lady with grey hair sitting in an armchair knitting away in the front room at the back of the village stores, by her feet lay a Collie dog with its head across her slippers.

Seemingly quite boring he turned and ran after his sister who was not waiting for him today.

Already, others on the island were well aware that the Beckett brother and sister were doing a little tour of the place.

The ravens were swirling and squawking in and out, up and down, shooting around the tree-tops in the forest like little spies they dived through the branches.

Septimus Dread decided to lock up his cabin and have a walk up to the old lookout tower. He took his powerful binoculars with him, the birds had alerted him to something, he wanted to go have a look. They were a bit like barking dogs on guard.

Mr Spangles stretched and arched his back up, and then down again. Jumping from the back of the chair he made his way over to a bowl that was tickling his taste buds, full of fresh fish it was. A nice bowl of full creamy milk was lapped up soon afterwards.

He already knew of the plans today to go

exploring, nothing got past his keen ears especially as he had spent the night prowling around and inside and outside of No.1 Waters End. There was no rush after all, a cat that could literally fly through the trees would take no time at all silently escorting two youngsters.

The barn owls were perched inside the barn roof. Apart from a quick peek by Tom Beckett the morning after they arrived nobody had been in the barn proper as yet, so they had remained undisturbed flying out at night snatching small prey to feed upon.

The only company they had as per usual had been visits from Spangles stealthily creeping around every night. *Too wit too woo*, they acknowledged him being there, all nocturnal creatures of the night.

The night owls were also small night watchman. A close enough distance to wisely see but not be seen by others, they were very camouflaged in their surroundings and were little lookouts and informers should the need arise.

They were trained to fly to Beanie if there were any signs of trouble. Trouble meaning the vampire bats that lurked deep in the hidden caves. As yet the bats had not been given any need to leave their side of the island.

"If I do say so myself Mrs, we are doing a very good job here." Tom stood back and admired their handiwork, they had achieved a lot since they arrived. The roof and chimney were now repaired, sealed and leak free, the loft had been insulated well. A small amount of plastering and making good on the inside walls was all it took on the upstairs of the house.

Grace agreed, they were working as a team on the painting. She was using a roller on the walls and Tom was doing the cutting in. The first room was almost complete, Mason's bed and furniture was all in the middle of the room. Next would be Scarlett's and even with two coats it should be dry just after lunch.

Yes, everything was nicely going to plan.

"Oh for goodness sake," Scarlett shouted. Mason was lying face down in the sand after tripping over a lump of driftwood as he was busy zooming in on his binoculars on a sign he spotted in between the trees.

"Why can't you watch where you're going?" she scolded him while grabbing his backpack to pull him back up.

"Are you okay?" came a voice behind them. Beanie was walking towards them.

"I'm alright," said Mason, dusting down his army style combats. "Who are you?"

"My name is Adam Stone, but you can call me Beanie, everybody does. I live here at No.3 and I look after all the animals on the island, I take it you are Scarlett and Mason from the big house?"

"Pleased to meet you," Scarlett said. "Big house? Is that what you call No.1?"

Beanie laughed, "Yes it's always been called that, well if you look at the others they're all a lot smaller. This one is me," he said, and pointed.

The game-keeper's lodge was really like the size of a very large garden shed to look at from the outside, but it did have an upper level too and an upstairs window with a balcony area overlooking the sea.

32

Outside was a circular seating area all made of wood, centred around a tree in the middle.

There was a hutch in the small garden with a run and inside there was a couple of small rabbits, black with floppy ears.

Mason walked over to them. "What's their names?" he asked, fascinated at them hopping about.

"These here are Bunny & Clyde," said Beanie. "And I do think that there will be some baby rabbits real soon too!" he smiled.

Mason freaked out when a couple of chickens came round the corner. "Ugh no," he shouted, looking worried.

"They won't hurt you!" Beanie laughed. "Where you both off to? I was just on my way to check on the sheep, it's on the way, I will walk with you."

"Just exploring the place a bit," replied Scarlett, glad of the distraction of a third person and a bit of mature company along the way. Mason looked back at the sign again through his binoculars.

'Danger-sinking sand.' Whoa, he thought, sinking sand? Really? Well it might not hurt to have a look one day, just to test it out a bit, just to see how really sinky it really is, like if it was that really sinky that I got stuck and couldn't get out, or if I really sunk low in it, but could get out. But what if I really couldn't get out and I was stuck in it? He was on a *get out of sinky sand mission* in his head now.

Mr Spangles noticed the three figures walking along the beach, seeing that Beanie was one of them he knew that Scarlett and Mason Beckett were in safe hands. It had been a busy night so he settled down at the bottom of a tree and drifted off to sleep.

It had been nearly two and a half hours now and as Beanie had gone off to tend to his sheep, Scarlett and Mason settled themselves down on grassy sand for a well earned rest and a little bit of a picnic. It was an autumn day but a very fine one, the temperature was around 13-14 degrees and they were quite warm after all the walking.

They sat looking out to the sea and both were quiet while they ate. Scarlett was taking in the view and realising just how beautiful this place actually was.

Why did it have a name like Witchetty Waters? She was intrigued to find out. Her trip to the mainland would involve joining the town library.

Mason was daydreaming. What was needed here were large ropes in the trees, he visualised himself swinging through them like Tarzan... avoiding sand that you could sink in, swamps probably, maybe an odd crocodile, even chickens. And a tree-house was on the list quick smart too.

The last house had been quite a bit further up. It would be No.7 Waters End and the occupant of that was the medic Basil Greenleaf, but Scarlett had decided that they should turn back now and maybe cut through a path in the forest.

As far as she knew there was a stream in the centre and if they could find that, it pretty much ran all the way back.

She looked at her watch, it was 12.15 so they should be back around 2 p.m. as planned.

Mason grabbed her by the arm, "Here you go Sis," he gave her one of the walkie talkies. "Just in case," he grinned.

They were going to be separated very soon, as it happened.

"I need the toilet," he said. "I will catch you up."

"Can you not wait for an hour?" she protested, but he had darted off before she could stop him.

She waited where she was for a few minutes and then called out to him, "Mason, Mason where are you?"

There was no reply. She walked deeper into the trees and kept calling his name. Mason had walked back in the direction he thought his sister was waiting but he couldn't find her.

"Scarlett, Scarlett," he called, but no answer.

Both carried on walking in different directions. Mason was using his compass and heading West, Scarlett was looking and listening for a stream.

Mason remembered his walkie talkie and took it out of his pocket, he pressed the button down and called out to his sister.

Scarlett jumped when she heard her brother's voice and realised it was coming from her pocket. She took out her walkie talkie and answered him quickly, "Where are you, where did you go?"

"Don't panic," he said. "I'm a Boy Scout I know what to do."

"You are a cub Mason."

"Same thing," he said.

He thought for a moment, pretty sure he was going the right way, he checked his compass again. Knowing his sister, who was a girl after all, she would be going, well he was not sure where but he knew it would be wrong.

He looked up to the sky and remembered what he had been taught when camping. "Scarlett," he said, "look up to the sky."

"Why?"

"Just tell me what you see."

"Well, the sun is faint behind the clouds."

"Good," he said, "keep turning so that you are walking towards it." She turned a half circle. "That is the way I am facing and it's due West which is the way home."

"I am very impressed Mason," she answered. She was so nervous out here on her own.

"I have my pen knife, I will mark a large arrow on the trees as I go," he said, convinced that his sister was actually behind him now. "When you see one let me know on the walkie talkie." He was very pleased with himself.

Five minutes later Scarlett came through, "I have found an arrow Mason. Stop where you are and let me catch you up." Who was the silly little boy now eh? He smiled.

Scarlett realised that her brother was not as stupid as she thought he was.

Two more arrows and ten minutes later the pair were re-united. Thank goodness her little brother had brought his gadgets and that the sun had stayed visible to guide her.

"Cool, hey," he looked up at her, she rubbed the top of his hair messing it all up. "Let's get ourselves out of here, we need to find the stream," she said.

Although he was a foot shorter than her, she felt safe with him, he was like a little soldier today. They carried on walking for another thirty minutes and suddenly they could hear the loud squawking of birds high above the trees, lots of birds.

"Blooming heck Mason, let's get out of here." They started to run through the undergrowth scratching themselves on the way. The birds' screeching was getting louder and louder.

Suddenly it got lighter and they could see a clearing up ahead. "Keep running to that," shouted Scarlett. In the clearing was the lookout tower, in the lookout tower was Septimus Dread. He had patiently stayed up there all day, looking this way and that way, and now his patience had paid off. The dark ravens were on full alert.

Scarlett pulled up sharp and grabbed hold of Mason. "Shush," she put her finger to her lips, "look." And there in the clearing making his way down the wooden rungs of the tower was a giant of a man, and worse than that, a giant of a man with an axe.

Mason began to shake, and so did Scarlett. They walked backwards as quietly as they could and as quickly as their legs would go. Why oh why did she not take her brother back the way they had come? This was all her fault, she thought.

They darted behind a very large oak tree and

ducked down into the brambles trying to make themselves as small as possible. The birds were circling overhead, shrieking and squawking.

At that point both of them felt something solid underneath them. Scarlett pushed away the undergrowth and thorns and was surprised to see a round wooden circle of wood about two foot wide and with an iron handle.

They both pulled hard on the handle and lifted up the wood. Mason took his torch out, shining it down into the dark hole, they saw a small ladder. He went in and started to climb down, Scarlett followed behind him and as she did, pulled the wooden lid down after her.

Still whispering, Mason found the other torch in his backpack and gave it to his sister. It was very dark down here and on one side they could see a tunnel. They started to walk down the tunnel hoping it would take them somewhere that they could get out, anywhere away from the giant axe man.

Septimus was a little bewildered, the birds were still screeching, but he didn't know what they were screeching at. There was nobody out here, he would know, he would hear them snapping twigs, but there was nothing.

He walked straight past the oak tree without looking behind it, and started to head out of the clearing and made his way home. Darn, he had wanted it to be those kids, he badly wanted to scare them kids away.

He had no idea he already had.

For fifteen minutes they carried on walking carefully through the tunnel and all of a sudden it just stopped. There on the side was another ladder made of rope. Scarlett took the lead and pushed up on the wooden lid which opened quite easily, she took a big gulp of air and helped Mason get up.

They were in a small building with cold stone floors and a small window. Shutting the lid back down, they looked out and realised they were in an empty storage building.

The door was not locked and they stepped outside into the daylight. They were on the very edge of the forest.

"I think we just found ourselves one of the hidden tunnels that the island has," Scarlett told Mason.

"Cool, do you think we can go in the other storage huts and go down them tunnels?"

"What I think," said Scarlett, "is that we need to go home."

CHAPTER FOUR

Friday morning and Scarlett had been up bright and early, showered, eaten a hearty cooked breakfast and was busy with the finishing touches to her room. It looked so different to when they had moved in.

Delicate pale lilac and white was the colour theme, matching curtains and bedding, a small double bed, wardrobe, dressing table with large mirror, a huge deep piled mauve rug, a walk in cupboard, and lots of feminine accessories. Everything was in its place, tidy and fragrant of lavender.

Mason's room consisted of a bed, large chest, wardrobe, dresser and an even bigger walk in cupboard. A tent once more in the corner, pale green walls, and clutter in most drawers and under the bed. It smelled of socks.

Scarlett had decided it would be best not to mention that she had lost her brother in the forest yesterday, Mason agreed. He was looking forward to breakfast in bed for a week to make sure he forgot, and the promise of new batteries for his torches and for his walkie talkies.

Wide eyed newts and slippery eel
Make the choppy waters real
Stormy waters wind and rain
Reveal to us your gotten gain

Elvira was busy mixing many potions and finding the spells she needed. It was written in the stars, it had been foretold in the crystal ball, it was whispered in the wind.

The keepers of the secrets and the keys to unlock the gates of the other six islands that were part of Witchetty Waters were going to be found in times gone by, and they would be found by the chosen ones.

The chosen ones had been picked many years ago, an innocent girl and an innocent boy who had wisdom far beyond their years during the Middle ages.

With the knowledge of the 21st Century and all of the centuries passed from 1367 unto the present day, all their hopes lay with Scarlett and Mason Beckett.

A boy with magical powers and trickery not known before, and a girl with the wisdom of foretelling the future, who would be protected by the peasants as she helped change their lives for the better.

Scarlett would not be taken for a witch, as indeed she would be protected by the higher witches.

Percy Taterhill had long planned, waiting for when the time was right and when the children were of the right ages to move the Beckett family, whom he cared about dearly.

The time was now, he wanted to see the curse of the islands lifted in his life time. The treasures and monies that were stolen by the pirates, and indeed hoarded by the King distributed back among the folk they were stolen from.

There had been strange goings on in the 1400 and 1500s, the witches that had been enslaved and chained in the tunnels were blamed for causing a terrible storm which sunk The Jolly Sea ship and all on board.

Also, every bit of gold bullion jewel encrusted cups, solid silver and hoards and hoards of money had gone down with the ship. The money had been taxes taken from the poor people and stored there under the King's orders.

The King had disappeared also, two years later. Some say he was taken to Pontefract Castle, where he vanished.

Indeed he did vanish, but the reason he was never seen again was not because he had been forced to hand over his reign and been abducted by the future king's men.

They had spared his life and sent him over to France to live a pauper's life amongst the peasants that he had been taxing heavily. He had been amassing great wealth from England and from France from the land and from the ships.

From riches to rags was his punishment, and he should live out his days in poverty, not daring to make himself known. These were the rumours.

At least, so the stories told, for no matter where all

mortal men looked, after the great storm took the Jolly Sea ship and all those aboard, no treasures or monies had been found, it had gone.

Friday night fell and Spangles glided through the air. Way above the island he soared as the gentle winds behind him helped him speed along in the cold night air. From a distance all that could be seen were two cats eyes in the dark, moving at speed.

He passed over the island and headed out toward the second island in the group. The group of seven islands together made Witchetty Waters.

The second island was much smaller than Waters End and from above all that could be seen was trees, nothing else but thick trees. In the centre of the island were two solid iron gates. At the back of the island were steep cliffs.

The gates were shut together and stood eight feet tall. They were old and rusted but were not to be opened, there was no visible lock.

An invisible barrier formed a complete circle either side of the gates, if you walked up to it you could go no further, you would hit a force that stopped you in your tracks. There was only one way to open these gates, and the day they were fully extended, the invisible barrier would be no more.

You could not get in from around it, above it, or under it. It was cursed ground and protected by witchcraft.

Mr Spangles came in to land on the edge of the beach, expertly gliding to a soft landing in front of the 'runway'. Hundreds of jellyfish darted about the shallow waters rising up near the surface, their luminous umbrella shapes giving away the exact location that the stealthy cat was looking for. He always descended just past them, onto solid dry ground.

He landed and they swam away knowing their job here was done, a stream of bright lights slowly disappeared as they went lower into the ocean.

Each of the islands were quite unique, all had their own occupants, and equally their own part of the puzzle.

Islands two, three, four, five and six were bound together, each one different but all of them had an identical gate and an unbreakable barrier. Only the key bearers would be able to undo the gates and with that release, each barrier would dissolve away.

Collectively all would need to be released to break the curse that had stood for over hundreds of years… so far.

The keepers of this island were the Runners, and indeed they ran as fast as the wind without grace but with purpose. They flitted about with great speed running and running, in the sea, out the sea, in the trees, out the trees, in the tunnels, out the tunnels, up the trees and down the trees, down the beach and up the beach.

They ran all day and they ran all night and they had been left to guard this island by King Gregory the Great ruler of the *Realm of the clocks of time*.

The Runners were a rare breed:-

Height… 12-18"

Weight… 10-12kg

Eyes… Large almond shapes, capable of 360

degree vision, and night vision.

Nose... long and thin

Ears... large and bat like, very sensitive, can hear much more than humans

Hair... tufted

Fur... Camouflaged and water proof

Arms... long and monkey like

Feet... three toes and long claws.

Talkers... yes very fluent

Fliers... No.

Their mission:- To run around in shifts night and day and report anything suspicious to Mr Spangles. Their reports to date added up to... none.

Spangles meowed three times. All the runners skidded to a halt and ran out from behind the trees, scuttled down the trees, shot out through the tunnels and dived out of the sea, others burst out from under the sand.

Fifty runners stood in front of him, five rows of ten, reporting for duty.

"Chief runner please step forward," Spangles commanded.

The Runner with a collar and attached whistle moved two steps toward him.

"Anything to report... anything at all?"

"No nothing, nothing at all, not up trees or down trees or behind trees or in front of trees not in tunnels up or down nor in the waters or under the sand, Spangles Sir."

"Very good, back to your duties Runners," Spangles ordered.

In a blink of an eye, they were gone, scarpered away, leaving a rush of wind. Spangles stretched his legs, gave a yawn and padded towards the centre of the island.

For many centuries the cats with magical powers had been overseeing the temporary keepers of the islands. They made sure the islands were safe, that the treasures were safe and spellbound under the curse of the higher witches.

Spangles had fulfilled his duty here on the mortal plain for the last 14 years so far. Back where he descended from, he was timeless, as were the horses, the owls, and many other creatures whose real home was a faraway place, *The Realm of the clocks of time.*

He would go to the gates and circle the invisible barrier as was his duty. He would check all of the other islands too, but only by air, then disappear into the Portal of ticking tocking.

Saturday arrived at long last, the Beckett siblings had spent a quiet day yesterday mulling around No.1. Scarlett added the last finishing touches to her room giving it the female touch. She just needed a bit of trinkets now, her Dad had promised her a treat or two!

Mason had spent no time in his room, but plenty of time in his corner of the shed where he had basic tools and apparatus and most importantly, a wild imagination.

He had been banging away most of Friday morning, inventing his most important 'flash bang box'. Every explorer needed one of course and the purpose was to make as much noise with it as possible followed by a blinding light to scare off predators, anything of a threatening nature, and chickens.

He had already filled his 'school form' out, wasn't much to say really.

Full name:- Mason Lewis Beckett

Age:- 9 ¼, that was important

Height:- 4' 5", inches also important

Weight:- 5 stones 4lb

Special subjects:- Chemistry, Science, Woodwork, Metalwork

Hobbies:- Inventing, Magic tricks, Camping, Exploring, Problem solving

That about covered it, that was all he needed to write.

Scarlett had also completed hers on Friday:-

Scarlett Kay Beckett...

13 years and 11 months…

5' 2"…

7 stones 6 lb…

Reading, English, History and Geography, Mathematics, Arts and Crafts, Cookery...

Hobbies, 'See above'.

"Is everybody ready?" Grace Beckett was already in her coat and quite eager to get over to the mainland.

They drove onto the ferry, there was no point

going on as foot passengers today. A little drive around after lunch, Tom thought. He wanted to become familiar with the town.

It was a relatively short crossing and Mason stood looking over Scarlett's shoulder as she sat browsing over the shop directory of the Harbour town of Westings.

Hmmm... *'Contessa Alessa'* had caught her eye, the small advert showed some pretty crystals and other pieces. Also there was a newsagents, there were some magazines she needed to catch up on.

Mr Marvello's *'Illusion Confusion'* shop, well Mason had a few tricks up his sleeve, sounded just the place for a visit. "Cool," he said aloud.

Scarlett had approached her parents regarding getting a broadband connection as there was already a landline connection on the island, and was pleased that this was now being arranged.

They drove off the ferry and headed round the one way system to find a car park. Mason had his nose pressed against the window and had left childish drawings on the steam.

Percy Tatterhill had previously arranged to meet up with the Becketts for a spot of lunch (his treat) so the plans were to do a bit of shopping this morning, followed by lunch, then time for a drive out before catching the late afternoon ferry back.

Having parked the car, they began the short walk back into the centre of town. It was very 'Olde Worlde' in these parts with cobbled paths and steep side roads. They had decided to just shop in whichever shops turned up first en route.

As it went, the first port of call was '*Buoys the Newsagents*', the sign above the door read *Patrick Hinger.*

Mason decided to wait outside. A trade bike came along just at that moment and a teenage boy scooped the empty paper bag from the front of it having finished the delivery round and pushed the bike round the side of the shop.

A few moments later he came back, eyed Mason standing there and walked over to him. "Alright," he said, looking at the young lad, "not seen you around here before."

"No, our first visit, we just moved here about three weeks ago," Mason replied.

"Whereabouts do you live then, not seen you anywhere?"

"We live over on them islands, Waters End."

"Aha that explains it then. I went there once, it was closed." Mason laughed at him.

"I'm Darren, people call me Dazlin, anything you need you just come and see me, it's a bit limited around here."

"Thanks, I'm Mason, yep may take you up on that," he grinned.

Tom thought he would introduce himself to the Shop-keeper while his wife and daughter browsed around in the shop.

He soon wished he hadn't. "Hello there, Patrick is it? Saw your name on the sign outside," Tom said, "thought I would just introduce myself." Tom Beckett continued. He explained who he was and gave the names of the rest of his family.

"Moved onto the island you say?" Patrick raised an eyebrow. "Wouldn't catch me over there on a dark night, I don't expect you've heard all the tales about that place? No, course you haven't cos if you had then you probably would not be living over there I expect," without pausing for breath he carried on, lowering his head he whispered, "haunted it is, haunted by pirates. People have seen them they have and that's a fact, cursed it is, cursed by witches. A long line of axemen have lived in the woods over there too, terrible place, terrible place."

He stood upright, once again returning to full volume. "Do you follow football Tom? We have a local team here *Westings Rovers*. Fat load of good they were last Saturday mind, they need to do better this afternoon."

"Ah, there you are Darren," Patrick was distracted, thank goodness. "Took your time boy," he said, looking at his watch, "they want their papers in the morning, not in time for afternoon tea."

Darren smiled shyly towards Scarlett, nodded his head at the others and walked through the back of the shop.

Marvello's '*Illusion confusion*' magic shop was the next place of interest, well it was to Mason. He made a bee line for the door, a large bell clanged when he entered. Dad went in the shop behind him. Mother and daughter sat this one out on the bench nearby.

Mason looked up all around him. Wow, he thought, it was cram packed, every shelf was full right up to the ceilings, and the large glass display counters were brimming with all sorts of everything and anything needed by a tricky nine year old.

Everywhere he looked was cards for magic tricks, cloaks, hats, wands, cups and dice, ropes, satin cloths, coins and magic tricks books, DVDs and much more.

After a few minutes there was still no sign of Marvello so Mason made his way to a door at the back of the shop and knocked. There was no answer so Mason knocked again and pushed the door open. Sitting with his back to him working at an old long table was an old man with short white hair. So busy he had not heard or noticed him, Mason thought.

Without turning the old man said, "Hello Mason, I've been expecting you, please come over I have something here that I have been making especially for you."

"How do you know my name?" Mason asked. "We haven't met before."

"Aha! Any magician worth his salt would know exactly when a fine young Master of trickery was about to pay a visit! Allow me to introduce myself, '*Wizard Marvello the Great*' at your service." The old man stood and bowed and as he did his clothes changed from a dark blue suit into a fine patterned cloak together with a matching wizard's hat.

"Whoa!" said Mason. "How did you do that?"

Marvello chuckled, "More to this wizard than meets the eye hey, now come and look at this."

Mason walked over to the table which was covered with all sorts. A microscope, test tube rack full of test tubes, pestle and mortar, funnels, droppers, glass jars, forceps, glass plates, litmus paper.

On the shelf were chemicals, but not ones that he recognised.

"Fascinating things we have here young Mason. Now then this is what I have been making for you," and he handed over two pairs of insoles. "A little something to help you with a speedy escape, maybe from chickens," he winked. "Just pop them inside your trainers and give them a little go, there are a pair for your sister too. They have been dipped in a particular solution of mine, one part H20 to five parts Cheetahbeater. Now let's go and see what we have in the shop shall we? I'm sure there is something out there that you would like your Father to buy for you today."

He bowed, and once again he was dressed back in his blue suit.

"Good afternoon Mr Beckett, good day to you Sir. I am Marvello and your Son has just been telling me all about you and your family."

Mason looked surprised to hear this, he had not mentioned his family. Very tricky old man was Marvello, he thought. "May I suggest one of these hats? Maybe a wand, a black cloth and a deck of magic cards for the young Master of trickery?"

"Wouldn't I need a rabbit or something?" Mason asked.

"But of course, don't you remember Beanie has two rabbits Bunny and Clyde and very soon there will be baby rabbits. I'm sure that there will be a special one just waiting for you!"

He smiled at Tom, who smiled back.

Tom was pleased with everything they bought, he knew it would keep Mason busy for several hours and out of his hair for a little bit. He was relieved at the thought.

Mason had the two pairs of insoles in his pocket. He was going to offer his sister a race later just wearing his pair to see how fast he could really run before he gave the other pair to her.

Maybe he would bet her first that he could beat her in a race, he thought.

Scarlett and her Mum had been sitting waiting and chatting away, the next shop would be their turn and it was one they both been excited to visit. There was a black signpost that pointed the way towards the Library, it was all in the same direction.

This was a must for Scarlett who wanted to get membership cards. She expected there would be many books about the history of the local area and she couldn't wait to loan two or three out.

Sophia Bonetti was very much a fast talking lady originating from Italy. She had come over here many years ago to stay with her Grandmother who was the famous Contessa Alessa of Florence.

She had liked it here so much that she had stayed permanently and taken over her dear departed Grandmother's shop.

'Contessa Alessa' sold everything spiritual, crystals, gemstones, amulets, dream-catchers, a gothic range plus Buddha's, oils, worry dolls, jewellery, boxes, bags, rugs, joss sticks, rock salt, lamps. It was an Aladdin's

cave to suit all tastes.

Grace and Scarlett entered the shop and a delicate little bell which hung over the inside of the door let out a little ding.

Sophia came out through a doorway behind the counter that had orange voiles draped over a silver beaded curtain.

"Good morning," she smiled at them, "please feel free to browse around the shop." Watching them she had a feeling that this must be Mrs Beckett and her daughter. She felt that she knew them after her long chat with Percy the other evening.

She also had a welcoming 'gift' for both of the Beckett children at the back of her shop. She went and retrieved the little package.

This place was just such a wow and both Grace and Scarlett were just fascinated at all the beautiful things that adorned the display cases. They had a feeling they would be some time in here.

"Are you new to the area?" Sophia asked Grace.

"Yes we live over on Waters End Village, the island across the channel, this is our first time on the mainland."

"Ah I thought so, I had not seen you here before," Sophia smiled. "I am sure you will love it, both the island and the mainland."

In no time Grace had filled a basket up. There was so much here to brighten up their house. She had a beautiful rose quartz crystal, a fruit wood zebra, a small rug and an owl planter. Scarlett had dropped in a small Indian box for her trinkets, scented candles and a leather bracelet.

They went to the counter, paid for the goods and were pleased to have them in intricate large decorated paper bags with handles.

"A small gift for you both," smiled Sophia. "Bellisimo," she said and handed Grace a silk head scarf, and to Scarlett she gave a small wrapped box. "Silver and black tourmaline," she said, "to protect you and keep you safe."

Scarlett thought the Italian lady had a look in her eyes that showed a bit of concern, she shrugged off the thought and accepted her gift with many thanks.

It would only be later when she opened the package that she would find not one, but two silver rings in the shape of skulls with insets of two black eyes of precious stone. There was a hand written note which read, *One ring for the girl with the power of foretelling and one ring for the boy with the power of trickery.*

She had no idea what that was all about. Strange folk around these parts, she thought.

CHAPTER FIVE

Septimus Dread was living up to his name. He had seen that family going off today and knew he had a few hours before the ferry came back later that afternoon. He would be leaving them a few welcome back 'surprises', together with a supply of logs for the week.

There was a bit more on his truck that day than yew logs. He was sure them kids had been in the forest, something was starting the Ravens off. Them places were his, they didn't have any business poking their noses around the Forest, or the caves.

When the day came that the treasures would be found, it would be by him, no-one else. He was staking his claim to that all right.

He would make their lives a bit more uncomfortable, he grunted as he stepped out of the truck and jumped down onto the leafy garden.

Tipping the truck down at the back he had opened the log store and was emptying the load of logs straight into the open shed space.

He made sure to look all about him as he was doing it to be certain there were no prying eyes as he made his way to the front of the truck and opened the passenger door.

This oughta give 'em a few frights tonight to be going on with, he thought, taking out big wooden boxes.

Inside the first box were Cardinal spiders in jars with small holes in the lids. He had carefully been collecting these for the last two weeks.

The next box had slow worms in it, big old things these were. He had been fattening them up, anybody that didn't know any better would mistake them for snakes, he had a fair few in the box.

A half a dozen field mice were also in his collection.

Toads, that's what he had in the last box, a dozen of them, and he was gonna let all these critters loose into the house so they had plenty of time to spread themselves around.

He went around the back of the house and using the cat flap that had long been in the bottom half of the door he dropped the slow worms first, followed by the toads, then the mice, and lastly he tipped out the jars of massive spiders. Nothing here was dangerous, he didn't intend to harm them, just scare the pants off them! Well the kids at least, and maybe the mother.

He chuckled to himself, got in his truck and drove along the beach, back towards the wood storage building.

Percy Tatterhill had met up with The Beckett family

at just after noon, they had finished their shopping expedition and taken their bags back to the car.

All things magical, mystical and readable.

They had also joined the town Library and the very knowledgeable head Librarian Mrs Cecily Springbocker had armed Scarlett with three large hard backed books. '*Westings through the ages*', *Ancient local folklore*' and '*Witchetty Waters*'.

The Coach & Horses Inn was way old looking, Mason thought. No music, no sports, no pool table, no machines, it was just a pub! A boring pub.

He noticed Dazlin Darren sitting in the restaurant end with his Dad. Darren put his hand up to him. Mason liked him, most older kids in his old town just ignored nine year olds.

Darren smiled at Scarlett, she smiled back, and blushed. Ugh! Thought Mason.

The two followed Percy and their parents and all got seated in the restaurant area too. They all picked up the menus and browsed.

Patrick Hinger had noticed them all, wiped his face with a napkin and walked over. They mostly tried to avoid eye contact with him. "If you want my advice," he said and bending forward so that everybody could hear him loud and clear, "you should stick to something off the specials board, least you know its fresh today, especially the fish. Well, can't hang around here talking, got a busy afternoon."

And with that he was gone, leaving his son sitting alone to finish his meal, already busy moaning away outside the window to no-one in particular. Percy lowered his head, "Patrick Hinger, the local whinger!" he whispered. They all smiled.

Percy called over, "Darren bring your plate over here and join us lad." Darren smiled and came over, sitting himself down next to Mason.

Everyone enjoyed sitting, relaxing and chatting over the next hour or so. Tom was updating Percy on the work he had been doing at the island, and Grace was joining in on the conversation. Scarlett, Mason and their new friend Darren had made their way up to the end of the table.

Every now and again they laughed a lot about Mason's antics and the stories Darren was telling them about a lot of the local people. It seemed Darren knew just about everyone and everything and had already promised Mason he could help him out with an old satellite dish and other bits and pieces.

Scarlett found him really easy to talk to and their shyness seemed to have disappeared. Already the three of them chatting like long lost friends.

He gave them his telephone number and email address for when they were online in case they needed him for anything. After another hour they all parted company having made plans to meet up soon.

The Becketts went back to their car for a little drive around the area before heading back on the ferry. They had all thoroughly enjoyed their day, so far.

Mason thought about the insoles in his pocket once again. "How do you fancy a little run along the beach when we get back?" he asked Scarlett.

"If you like," she shrugged.

Mrs Bakewell had been sitting in her favourite chair that afternoon, knitting away. Busy with bobble hats she was, little gifts for Christmas time for the new children at No.1.

She had a very beady eye, two of them in fact and was more than capable of knitting away, watching TV and keeping an eye of everything going on nearby. Although to anyone passing by she was just a dear old lady sat in her armchair, oblivious.

Septimus Dread had not escaped her line of sight and she knew he had no business poking around the house for so long. He was a very strange man she knew, and not to be trusted. He wasn't the sharpest pencil in the box which gave his actions away, whatever he had been lurking about doing.

She thought the family should be told about his visit.

Time to open the shop up, she thought and say hello to her new neighbours. The ferry would be on its way back she knew. She switched on the bright lights to light up the porch and went outside to the blackboard.

~Freshly baked today ~
Poppy seed bread
Crusty rolls
Cheese & onion flan
Chocolate cakes
Apple turnovers
~

The smell that wafted out of the kitchen that afternoon was irresistible. Coffee was percolating, the teapot was warming up and special milkshakes were being blitzed. Mr Bakewell was mooring up the little boat for the night, a pleasant afternoon fishing. He took his catch and made his way home to wash and clean up.

Mr Spangles was in the other Realm at this moment in time. *The Realm of the clocks of time* was a magnificent Paradise, where all planning was carried out to precision, where all events were logged at leisure. The planning of time and space was foretold hundreds of years in advance, nothing happened by chance, it was all fated to be.

As was the approaching time for Scarlett and Mason to start the chain of events that much depended on.

Spangles flew over the '*Almost time*' area and floated down amongst the members of the Wise Council. The members of the council were hundreds of years old, all of them having long white hair. The only difference between the gentlemen and the ladies was that the men also had long white beards.

They had long flowing robes that were also white, and each one had a long chain around their necks made of the purest gold and hanging on the end of these were gold watches, the council of the clocks of time.

The council sat at a table that was so long you could not see the end of it, filled with papers in many piles each weighed down with a huge golden paperweight. There was a bright light that surrounded each and every thing. The ladies wore a circle of small flowers on top of their heads.

King Gregory the Great was a fair and just ruler of the *Realm of the clocks of time*, He left his wise council to oversee any wrongs that had been done on Planet Earth that needed to be rectified so that the line of fate could be put back on course and wrongs that could be righted would be made right.

They did their best to make sure that Good always triumphed over Evil, where they could.

So, if that meant going back in time and changing events that were not destined to happen because they caused a string of distress, then they would use their powers to re-write history. It was not easy and involved a lot of planning and years and years of thought.

There had been six such errors that had not been written into the time line of events as they should have happened. A group of seven Islands that were situated off of the Kent coast which were meant to have been used as sanctuaries for orphans, the homeless, disabled, animals, white witches, healers and holy pilgrims.

Instead only one island had been used, for the wrong reasons and six islands had been left cursed, hiding treasures.

It was the job of the Wise Council to go back to the times this all took place and change the course of history, to right the wrongs. With the right two people who possessed knowledge hundreds of years in advance plus wit, magic, courage, trickery, and the power of fore seeing the future, the plans were all in place.

The plans that depended on Scarlett and Mason, the time was now right to change this first particular course of history.

Spangles bade his farewell, left his empty reports, from each and every island and made his way over to the swirling portal of mauves, white and gold. He walked into it and was transported back to Witchetty Waters.

Two others also walked into the portal, magnificent horses of pure black and dapple grey. They would be transported back to the top of the hill on Waters End, where they watched. They too would be needed soon.

The Becketts arrived back and drove from the ferry and onto Waters End. As they approached they noticed a man flagging them down to pull over.

Tom wound his window down, and as he did they all could smell such wonderful aromas coming from the village store.

"How do, I'm Ted Bakewell. My wife and I would like for you to come and have a spot of tea with us, if you fancy?" Mason was nodding very quickly, Tom and Grace thanked him.

How could they refuse, even after such a substantial lunch, the smell was very enticing. Tom parked the car and they all got out and headed into the little store.

Scarlett stretched out her legs and patted her stomach. Little race after tea, she thought. They were soon tucking into all sorts, freshly baked bread buttered with ham and cheese, big crusty roll for Tom, and very tasty cakes and pastries.

Nancy was very pleased to watch them enjoying her fare, and Grace insisted on buying a bag full to take home too.

"Would you like to come and have a look around Tom?" Ted pulled his arm and gave Tom a look that suggested it was not so much of a request more like a command.

Tom and Ted went for a stroll around the garden, leaving the two ladies to chat. Mason had inserted his insoles slyly and him and his sister were just waiting a bit to let their food go down before they would run along the beach.

It was soon apparent that Ted had not taken Tom out just to show him his organic gardens. "I don't want to worry you," he said, "but my good lady wife told me that Septimus, the wood man, had been hanging around the back of your house for some time this afternoon after he delivered your logs. The wife saw him with boxes going around the back.

"Now," he went on, "Septimus has been on the island for a good many years. He used to live with his Uncle before he passed away, and as far as I know he is not a well educated man, neither was his Uncle. Cutting logs is all he has ever known and carried on after his Uncle who was the Lumberjack around here for many years too.

"Thing is," Ted paused as he looked directly into Tom's eyes, "although not a dangerous man, he is not to be trusted, not at all, and he is up to something in the woods, mark my words. No idea what but he is always lurking around, and I've noticed since you arrived a fair few signs have gone up around the place, warning signs.

"You need to keep an eye on your children, best they stay away from him, the woods and the hidden bay at the back of the island. And I tell you why that is," he carried on, "it's because it is haunted, that's why, seen them myself, Pirates, in all their ghostly glory."

Tom listened intently to everything he had been told. "Tell you what Ted I think it may be a good idea to go and have a look around the house before the others go back there don't you?"

"Exactly my thoughts," Ted replied. Pirates? thought Tom.

Maybe best when Scarlett and Mason started their tutoring he had a good proper look around the place himself.

"Alright alright," Scarlett said, "I'm coming." Why Mason was so eager to be beaten by her, yet again she had no idea, but she would humour him.

"Tell you what," she said, "if you like I will give you a head start."

"No, no, I will give you a head start," Mason was grinning broadly.

All that milkshake has gone to his head, she thought, been watching too many superhero movies again.

They walked to the grassy area of the beach and looked ahead for the finishing spot. It was decided that they would race to a very large tree in the distance that stood out high above the others.

Scarlett walked several yards ahead, and turning

back she smiled at Mason. He put his thumbs up. "Ok," she shouted out, "on your marks, get set, go."

She quickly picked up pace and raced off.

"Okay Cheetahbeaters let's see what you can do." He took in a big breath, arms ready, he charged off. "Woohoo," he shouted and just took off like a bullet, swept straight passed Scarlett like a bat out of hell and cleared around 400 meters in around 20 seconds.

He had literally knocked Scarlett off her feet as he raced passed, and he was no longer in sight. All she could see was him in the distance jumping around in a victory dance.

Before she could get herself up off the floor, Mason had already raced back to her. "Oh my God," he said, "this is so wicked."

"What the heck just happened here?" she asked, staring at him. He must have sprinted at the speed of a fast car. His feet hardly touched the ground, whoosh he had gone and whoosh, straight back again.

Mason sat down beside her and paused for breath. "Look," he said, and pulled his trainers off, showing her the insoles. "When I went into Marvello's '*Illusion Confusion*' shop with Dad, the old guy was at the back, and it was like he knew me and knew I was coming already without even looking at me."

Scarlett remembered back to having the same feeling with Elvira Vickery when she had visited them. She knew she was at the top of the stairs without even looking!

"Well anyway, he told me he had made something for me, and something for you too." He handed the other pair of insoles to Scarlett. "Cheaterbeaters they are, dipped with a special solution, they will get us out of tricky situations when we need them," Mason explained hurriedly. "Just look at the other day in the forest, we could have got out of there so quickly!"

"I was given a gift as well," she said and took the package outside of her inside pocket and opened it. Inside were two silver rings. They were the shape of skulls with black stones for eyes. "Wow," she said.

"Wicked," said Mason.

"They are meant to protect you, Mrs Bonetti told me, protect you from what I have no idea, but here you go."

She gave the smaller of the rings to her brother, both fitted perfectly, and she put the insoles into her trainers too.

"Ready?" she said.

"You bet," Mason said, and they ran.

They ran and they ran and they laughed so loudly as they ran, shooting past everything in the blink of an eye. Neither of them noticed that the eyes in the matching rings were glowing. They were, unbeknown to them, charging them up with the kick start energy needed for their protection to start.

"*And so it has begun,*" whispered Spangles, watching them from the rooftop. The horses stood atop the hill watching them, they reared up and neighed. Many little eyes stopped still and ears pricked up on the second island, the runners could hear the rushing of the winds being caused. At long last they would have something to report, they were very excited.

Grace and Nancy Bakewell were sat chatting away on the front porch of the village store, swapping recipes, and having a good old chat about anything and everything. Nancy had shown Grace the bobble hats she was knitting for Scarlett and Mason. *Special* bobble hats.

> *Rushing winds and eyes of night*
> *Days of old in our sight*
> *Lizards tongue stir the pot*
> *Make it fiery make it hot.*

Elvira Vickery was hastily preparing many spells, not long now she thought. The two men had just entered No.1 Waters End, not at all sure of what they might find.

CHAPTER SIX

As it happened, when they had left the house earlier, Tom had shut all of the downstairs doors. It was a habit of his.

Nothing was apparent when the men walked into the front door of the house. Everything was as it was left, no funny smells, fire or water, no break in, they opened doors and looked inside. As they approached the kitchen they could hear a funny noise.

"That sounds like toads if I'm not mistaken," said Ted. Tom slowly opened the door, and there they were, toads, slow worms, mice, jumping, sliding and running on the floor.

Tom quickly shut the door again to contain them. He was very angry and ranted at Ted, "What the heck does that man think he was doing? Grace and Scarlett would have a merry fit if they come back and saw these."

Mason would probably think it was very cool, but that was beside the point.

"You stay here, I will go and get Beanie. He will be able to get rid of them for you, sharpish." Ted left the house. Tom's mind was racing, how had Septimus got in? Everything was locked, and why would he do that?

He closed the front door and went around the house, the log shed had been filled up, then he went around the back. He noticed a jar there on the floor next to the back door, it had not been there before.

Kneeling down, the penny dropped. He pushed against the cat flap and it opened, it was lockable from the inside, he had forgotten to do it.

High on his work list now would be locks on the inside of all the windows, inside the outside doors to the cellars, extra security on the doors, and maybe even an alarm. He would tell Grace that it was all necessary for house insurance on a property this remote.

Beanie was straight there and he had special pet carrying boxes with him.

"Hello Tom," he said. "Ted has told me what's happened, let's get these little creatures out of the way for you."

The other two men stayed outside. "Cowardly nasty thing to do," Ted said.

"But why would he do it?" Tom answered.

"Oh that's simple," Ted replied. "He wants you out, he wants us all out."

A short while later many mice, slow worms and toads had been released back into the forest. There was only two occupants more at No.1 Waters End, two very large spiders on the loose, hidden from sight.

One floor wash and kitchen spruce up later, the house was locked and the two men resumed their walk back towards Ted's garden as if they had been there all the time. They were now deciding on the best course of action of how to deal with Septimus Dread.

Scarlett and Mason had come to a stop at long last, quite exhausted. "That was the most amazing thing, ever," Mason said. "He really is a very tricky old wizard."

"I think we should keep this as our little secret Mason don't you?" Scarlett stared at her brother. "I'm not sure why but I just get a funny feeling about things, a feeling right down in my stomach that something around here is a bit well, not spooky, but strange." They both agreed on that.

"Yep, it's way cool though," Mason said. They agreed on that too, stood up and walked back, their legs ached.

It had been quite late when the Beckett family had arrived home that Saturday night after a pleasant evening spent with Ted and Nancy Bakewell. Firstly out on the front porch and then in the back room, sitting around the big log fire and Scarlett and Mason laying on the floor along with Alfie the old Collie dog.

Many tales had been told to them last night about the islands, the folk that had come and gone, the history of the islands and much more.

Ted and Nancy had left out some of the more scary parts, but no need because all of it was written in the library books that Scarlett had bought back with her on loan. She would soon be reading all about it, in fact she would start reading in bed later, she thought.

Tom was relieved that when they went back there was no sign of any more reptiles or mammals about the place, and the floors and surfaces were all clean and dry.

"You were right love," Ted told his wife, "that man had been up to no good again."

She shook her head. "Something needs to be done about him," she sighed.

There was a new addition to the island overnight once Ted had taken it upon himself to give Percy Tatterhill a late evening telephone call.

A special delivery collected by Ted himself halfway out across the channel where the two small sea boats met each other.

A Dragondoggen, one of these creatures had not been seen, well not been seen ever really. It did not descend from around here, it had been transported by a special portal delivery via the Deep dark cavern of Westings, in a part roped off from any prying eyes.

It stood on large back legs with a tail that was strong, powerful and reptilian, its front legs were a lot shorter. The back of it had strong ridges that stood up. It was dark green. That's where the lizard like reptile ended and the shoulders and the head were that of a Newfoundland dog, but also dark green.

This was Dino, who was not your average house pet. He was especially trained, his speciality was whip lashing intruders with his mighty tail, plus a little singeing with his fire breath if and when necessary.

On the lighter side he would be very friendly to his owners and all people of good intention, nothing he liked more than a good head rub.

He was the ideal Dragondoggen... watch dog dragon type to watch and protect the new islanders.

Also that night a few other creatures dropped in. Up high in the treetops all over the forest were sprites, that is to say fairies, elves and goblins. Not just your usual sprites but the supreme ranking immortal helpers and wish givers of the highest degree.

The sand duners were very busy, when they heard the rushing feet and felt the high winds above them the afternoon, before they knew it was time to spring into action. Tricky little creatures no bigger than pixies, and very naughty. They were the trap setters and capturers of all bad intentions.

No.2 Waters End was no longer a storage facility, overnight it had become home to Night watchman Freddie Spinner. He worked all night and he slept all day, but mostly he told lies. He lied all day long each and every day, it was his speciality. He never told the truth about anything, ever.

Percy had been aware that Septimus Dread had spent many fruitless years searching for treasures on Waters End, he would never find them there of course because they weren't there!

Up until now he had been a bit of a deterrent, his reputation in these parts as a mad wood man with an axe had at least stopped attention being drawn to the islands, as had his Uncle before him.

Times were changing now and it was time to drive Septimus away from Waters End, it would be best for the big man to think it was his own decision to leave.

Percy had plans for all seven islands and Waters End would be the main hub serving the other islands. Freddie Spinner would be a big help in the evacuation of Septimus Dread, as would the sprites now dwelling in the forest.

Septimus had thought he would sleep well over Saturday night, he also thought that the family at No.1 would have been so alarmed at a house full of outside creatures they would be packing their bags. He would be wrong on both counts.

Sunday morning and Scarlett had been up early, Tom and Grace were still sitting up the kitchen table chatting away with plans for the house. Mason was busy perfecting one of the best magic tricks with cards he had ever seen.

"Shush, what's that?" Tom asked Grace. "There it is again." A large whooshing noise was heard just outside the back door.

There was a knock on the kitchen window and Ted was standing there giving a little wave. Tom opened the door and nearly fell straight back in again. What the heck was that?

Stood outside and staring right at him was a creature that was nothing like he had ever seen before! "Don't be alarmed Tom," Ted laughed. "This is Dino, Dino the Dragondoggen, all the way especially imported from," he paused, "from a faraway place. Meet your new guard dog, well, bit of a cross breed admittedly!"

Grace stood up and looked outside. "Oh my gosh," she gasped, not at all sure what she was looking at.

"Don't worry," Ted said, "he is very friendly and

loves nothing more than a pat on the head." Ted demonstrated this to them both, in return he got a big fat lick across his face, he laughed.

"Don't you be fooled mind, if you were ever to get any intruders up to no good, he will see them off for you." He gave Tom a wink.

"Jolly good idea," Tom replied. "Welcome to our home Dino." Wait till the kids see this, he thought, and off he went to call them.

"He is not particular Grace, he will eat anything, meat, fish, vegetables, you name it, and he will do just nicely settled about in the outside barn. He isn't your average domestic pet."

Grace was a little relieved to hear that, it could be rather messy, she pondered.

Dino nudged his way into the barn. Circling around and around he quickly found his corner. *"Perfect place for a Dragondoggen as long as I don't breathe fire in here."*

"Oh yes, I forgot to mention," said Ted, "he talks too, bit broken mind but you can understand him alright."

"Things just got a whole lot trickier around here," Mason said. They all stared at the creature.

Septimus had not slept, not slept at all. All night long the ravens had been screeching and screeching, they hadn't stopped. Three times he had gotten himself out of his bed and gone outside

He had taken his axe with him the last time, swinging it about and making large grunting noises in all directions.

He couldn't see anything, what were those darn birds making such a fuss about? It was quiet, strangely quiet in fact. No night owls twit too wooing, no wind blowing around, no creatures snapping twigs, twas all in all silent, very silent.

Except for the ravens, he covered his ears at the noise they were making. He cursed them for screeching, they swooped down and back up again circling and screeching, never stopping.

He made his way to the clearing in the early morning hours and went up the wooden ladder in the lookout tower. It was too dark to see out of the binoculars. He sat on the wooden floor and waited, it was cold and quiet, eerily quiet, only the ravens, his ravens, were stirred up.

The elves, the fairies, the goblins, all of them tiny little creatures were making merry in the tree tops. The fairies were busy spinning thread so strong from leaf to leaf and branch to branch, and the elves and goblins were attaching thick moss and resin from inside the branches making little runways all over the place.

As the day started to break they made their way inside the trees to settle down to rest, there they would stay until nightfall, and start all over again. They had many nuts and berries in little stores to feast upon. The magical waterfall was now once again running into the forest streams which had dried up. They now drank the purest water ever tasted on the Earth.

Their shenanigans had stirred up the dark black birds, and the ravens had soon found that they could not get anywhere near these strange small creatures as their bright fairy lights shone straight into the birds' beady eyes, blinding their sight every time they tried to swoop.

The sprites were here to deprive Septimus of his sleep every night until he could take it no more, forcing him to flee and take his dark ravens with him.

Daylight came and the forest returned to normal, the ravens were silent, the animals scurried around the forest floor, the sprites were retired for the night.

Septimus had just started to doze in the tower, cold and shattered, he snored loudly. An hour later he would be woken again by Freddie Spinner.

Scarlett and Mason were both gobsmacked by Dino. "Told you this place was tricky," Mason whispered.

Scarlett whispered back, "Exciting isn't it though? I know something is afoot around here, nothing is as it seems."

Dino the Dragondoggen, thought Mason. Charlie will never believe all this when I tell him. "Scarlett?"

"Yes?"

"Can you get your ring off?"

Scarlett pulled the skull ring, but it wouldn't budge, it would not even turn on her finger. "No, it won't move," she said.

"Neither will mine," said Mason. They gave each other a puzzled look.

Elvira Vickery had quietly slipped them a note through the front door telling them what they would need to bring to lessons at 9 o'clock sharp Monday morning.

CHAPTER SEVEN

Freddie Spinner paid Basil Greenleaf a little visit to collect some herbal tea bags to aid in his restful daytime sleep, and whilst he was about it he would put together a special flask brew for Septimus that mainly consisted of a touch of tea leaves and a fair amount of laxatives.

"Just one or two is all you need to loosen up your bowels man," Basil advised.

"Terribly constipated I am," lied Freddie. "A dozen or so to keep me going I think." That raised an eyebrow, and a smile.

He knew he would find the big man either in his cabin or up in that tower of his, shouldn't be hard to find. The sound of heavy snoring led him straight to the clearing.

Making his way up the wooden ladder he was going to make sure Septimus would be wide awake and log chopping. In actual fact he now had a massive load to chop up today that was going to the mainland, an urgent order, but it would be okay, he had plenty of tea to keep him going. "WAKE UP MAN," he shouted, right next to his head.

Scarlett and Mason did not question their 'school list' and neither did their Mother. Once the seeds had been planted by the suggestive scones supplied by Elvira Vickery, the affects would be ever lasting until such time that the un-suggestive spell was chanted and the neutralising spiced tea cakes had been eaten. The school list read:-

Clothes of old and shoes well worn
Hoods and tights not too torn
Rings of skulls and feet of speed
Tricks and knowledge that's all we need
Horses ready end of day
Hocus pocus be on your way

The Beckett children gathered large bowls for their new cool 'pet' and they went out armed with cold water, lots of meat and a huge bone.

They hadn't actually been inside the barn as yet so decided to have a good snout around it today and tidy it up a bit for Dino the talking Dragondoggen. How way cool was he?

"*A large pile of straw heaped at this end would be most welcome,*" Dino said whilst he was busy slurping away at the water. Scarlett was paying attention, Mason however had found a ladder and was up into the rafters looking around.

Several pairs of eyes shot open and blinked repeatedly at him startling him. He came face to face with the Barn Owls all perched along the roof beam. "Woah," he said, staring at them, this place was full of never ending surprises!

"Scarlett," he shouted down. "There's a load of owls up here," and with that the smallest one flew over and landed on his shoulder, wisely watching all he was doing.

She heard him but had just uncovered a large wooden chest that had been hidden among the straw. Opening the heavy lid, she sneezed with all the dust and straw everywhere. Inside there was some really old sack clothes and strange shoes. "I think I just found our school list," she called back.

"Who are you?" Septimus looked up bleary eyed at this strange man in the lookout tower.

"Davy Dingle," Freddie lied. "Chief bottle washer and head cook."

He gave Septimus the flask and written order for very large lorry load of logs. "Soup," he said as Septimus stared at the flask, and he left the big man, bewildered and tired and headed back to get himself some shut eye with the help of his herbal tea mix.

Basil also had a special medical bag full of herbs and plants that had been chopped up and put in small plastic labelled bags. Anti-sickness, stings & bites, cuts, sleeping brew, antidotes for spiders snakes and vermin, anything and everything he could think of and he took it to Elvira.

He let himself in through the back door, he could hear her chanting away in the back room. The air was filled with all sorts of strange smells as the cauldron hubbled and bubbled away with a mysterious coloured liquid spluttering noisily.

"Elvira," he called out to her. She appeared, looking even more vibrant than usual, her eyes were a piercing green today and shining brightly. Her long fingers adorned long black painted nails, she was fully adorned in her witching robes.

"Getting all prepared?" he asked her. She looked very strange.

"Quite," she said. "Ah good I see you have brought the medic bag, never know what they might need. Exciting isn't it, we have waited so long for this, let's hope their first 'visit' goes to plan."

"More importantly," said Basil, "is that we can get them back again." She looked thoughtful and hoped so too.

Spangles left the house for a quiet little stroll around, all that witchetty stuff was leaving him quite light headed!

Making his way to Storage House No.2 he found the window open and there was Freddie Spinner sound asleep on the small pull out bed. He jumped onto the end of it and joined him for a few hours of peaceful slumber. It had been a busy night.

Septimus could hardly keep his eyes open, so he opened the flask and poured out a large cupful of soup. Didn't look like soup to him, still it was hot and it warmed him up.

Yuck! Strangest soup he ever had, none the less he poured another cupful and took it with him on the way to the back of the island to where the trees were to be chopped.

He was cold, tired and now he needed the toilet, he hurried his pace. The sand duners were all heading around to the back of the island as well, today would be fun, a lot of fun. They enjoyed being naughty, the naughtier the better.

"Ho heave ho."

"Pieces of eight."

"Shiver me timbers."

"Ahoy me hearty."

The Ghost pirates were all being noisy today in their troubled waters, on their ghostly ship The Jolly Sea. Sunken deep, they floated around it, rushing through it, passing straight through each other and through the waves. One or two had raised up out of the sea and circled around into the bat filled cave of hidden bay.

Out they went again and back down into the water, on an endless mission searching for their lost gold in their in-betweeny world, tormented souls being punished for their greed.

Today the dead pirates were extra sensitive and making a lot of ghostly noises.

All in all, Septimus Dread would not be having a very good time on this side of the island. The Ravens once again started circling everywhere and screeching, there was trouble in the waters, and trouble in the sands, they were on full alert.

Marvello the Great was busy with his next batch of chemicals and mixing up a concoction of H20 and Brighterlighter which was a ratio of two parts to six parts.

He would be soaking in this two pairs of almost transparent flesh coloured gloves. This special trickery power would cause a light so bright when the hands were rubbed together that one could become almost a human torch.

In an Olde Worlde so dark with no electricity, the uses would be many.

When he finished this, his next mixture he labelled Clearerhearer and for this he needed a mix of one part H20 to five parts.

Almost invisible ear pieces once dipped in this solution would enable you to hear anything within a three mile radius and was an essential item for listening for approaching enemies.

And so it went on, 'Bumperjumpers', when great height was needed these special bouncing kneepads would let you jump up to heights of twenty feet or more when activated from a kneeling position.

And Eyespy patches, worn over one eye these would increase your sight of vision to 360 degrees and for at least two miles all around.

Marvello would have all of these items ready once Scarlett and Mason had been on their first trial visit to the 1400s. Of course, they had no idea yet that this was to happen.

They would have the aid of light, sound, speed, agility and hearing, all superhuman, the protection of the higher witches and rings of protection. The rest would all be up to them.

Changes were happening in Waters End Forest. Scarlett would not have found the stream before it had been dried up for years, the images she had looked at were very outdated. Now though, the waterfall that had magically appeared in the centre of the forest was bringing with it fresh running brooks all over the place.

A haunting melody could be heard around the trees and it was looking different on this side of the island, it was becoming enchanted. Not so on the far side, the crawling ivy and ferns were slowly creeping their way up the walls of the log cabin where Septimus had resided for many years. The trees were growing thicker together, it was getting darker and darker.

Nancy Bakewell was adding finishing touches to the two Bobble hats. Winter was fast approaching and by the time those two children had been to'ing and fro'ing backwards and forwards, they would need plenty of rest in between.

Their minds would need resting, by the time it was Christmas they would surely be needing a break.

Her hats were just the thing, in the special blend of wool was a grounding dye giving the wearer peace of mind and a calming influence. Bit like a little brain cell holiday, an unthinking and unwinding festive period.

Mason was adding a little extra couple of things in his school bag for break time, a double headed coin, playing cards, beakers and a dice, a little bit of tricky time, on what was bound to be a boring day. Little did he know.

Scarlett was intrigued by the history of the island, deep into her book she was reading up about the great storm and the 'curse'.

The wind started to pick up very quickly on the island and the sky turned a very dark grey, a loud rumbling in the sky was quickly followed by sheet lightening. Moments later it rained fiercely and then it started to hail too, rapping loudly on the windows.

Scarlett sat on her bed looking out at the sky, where had that come from? Five minutes ago the sky had been clear, she had never seen so much rain fall so quickly and the hailstones were gigantic. Another very loud clap of thunder made her jump, she counted until the next lightening 1... 2... 3... 4... 5... then the room lit up brightly. Wherever this storm had suddenly come from it was almost on top of them.

Mason had his nose pressed to his bedroom window, "Excellent, well cool." The trees were blowing wildly and bending and the ground outside was covered in white.

Strange coincidence, Scarlett thought, that she had only just been reading about the great storm that sunk The Jolly Sea Ship and all on board, and then a storm whipped up from nowhere.

The largest bang of thunder roared out in the sky and Scarlett moved from on her bed to under it. She never had liked thunder, it scared her.

Her room lit up with the brightest light as the lightening followed straight afterwards. Hail was bang bang banging against the window and the wind was howling loudly.

The sea was whipped up into a frenzy and the high waves came crashing down at the water's edge and the small boats were violently jumping up and down in their moorings.

Amongst all of this sudden chaotic ferocious weather something dropped down from the sky and into the water at great speed and disappeared into the depths. As quickly as it had started it came to a sudden stop. The wind, rain, hail, thunder and lightening just stopped. The storm had passed.

A few moments later the sky was bright again with the winter sun and everywhere was calm and dry. It was as if the heavens had opened up and then closed the doors shut.

This 'something' that had dropped was certainly not heavenly and neither had it been anything to be of any assistance from *The Realm of the clocks of time*.

It was not a something nor a someone but an object, a mysterious object. And it had not dropped out of the sky by accident. It went deep down into the water and headed for a hidden underground cavern.

Nobody at all had seen it, nor knew of its existence. The only tell-tale sign that it was there was a green light deep down in the water and the hasty retreat of all marine life from the area.

A green light now pulsed deep in the ocean, beating in rhythm with a Mother Ship that took off sideways above the clouds and shot away at terrific speed and then stopped still. 50,000 feet altitude, it was above commercial aircraft flights but not yet into space territory.

An invisible barrier enclosed around it and it was not detectable by any radar, essentially a UFO, but it did not contain little green men. A time capsule would better describe it.

It would not be the first time that this had happened and probably would not be the last. In actual fact this was the real cause of the catastrophic weather which was indeed a raging storm that took down the Jolly Sea ship deep into the depths of the ocean.

And it did not happen by chance. The witches were blamed conveniently for the storm hence the naming of the islands into Witchetty Waters.

The only part that they played was to retrieve the treasures after it sunk, securing them on the smaller six islands and placing them under curse where they remained ever since.

There the treasures would stay and what real chance did a couple of kids have in changing so much that had happened hundreds of years before?

King Gregory, ruler of the *Realm of the clocks of time*, had a much stronger force to contend with in his quest to try and help those chosen to alter the history of time.

It was no secret to him that the *Time warp Ship of the sky* from the *Andromeda Galaxy*, a Universe parallel to Planet Earth, had the advantage of being able to travel faster than the speed of light, the only craft that ever could.

Its mission had not been to sink a ship back then, the ship just happened to be there. The purpose of dropping off of the box from outer space was to let it fall into waters not yet inhabited by alien life form, and there it would slowly release acids to form into a DNA.

Never seen on this planet before and multiplying into cells and gradually a life form. An alien life form the same as that living in the Andromeda Galaxy, yes there is life in another Universe far superior to ours! The purpose was to invade Planet Earth and take over.

Now it was apparent that time travelling powers were to be used by King Gregory from the *Realm of the clocks of time* together with helpers from this day, the *Time warp ship of the sky* needed to drop many more boxes of alien life through different moments in time to ensure the success of invasion and takeover.

In particular, the years 2016-2022.

The ship had no power to stop what would take place on the ground and through portals, its only means was time warping in the Universe. To change the course of years gone by could cause problems, many problems. Scarlett and Mason Beckett needed to be stopped.

Septimus Dread had gotten totally soaked through, it wasn't enough that he felt exhausted and had the most severe stomach upset, he still had to get all these logs down to that Chief cook Davy Dingle down by the storage facility.

Before the day turned to night, Septimus drove the truck filled to the brim with logs to the front of the island. Freddie Spinner had been up a short while after a lovely day's sleep and was seeing to some sizzling bacon and a large mug of tea. Mr Spangles was much rested too and had crept out of the window just as Freddie had begun to stir up awake.

Headlights beamed across the floor and Freddie looked out to see the truck approaching, he grinned to himself.

Going outside he asked Septimus what he wanted. "Your order of logs being delivered, what does it look like?" he barked.

"Logs? Sure I have no idea what you mean," Freddie lied. "I didn't order no logs."

Septimus took out the order form, *'Davy Dingle large lorry load of logs to be delivered today, urgently,'* it read. "Davy Dingle?" said Freddie. "Never heard of him."

The Sand Duners as if on cue came to the surface of the sand. *"This way, this way,"* their high pitched voices were all shouting the same thing at the same time. *"Over here, over here."*

What on earth was going on? Septimus rubbed his eyes staring out all around him. He could just make out small shapes darting around, nothing like this had he ever seen before. *"Follow me, follow me,"* their shrill demands shouted louder and louder.

"Let's go, let's go," as he walked toward them they scurried further away. *"Come on, come on."*

They were all over the place, he didn't know which way to go. The noisy little 'things' were totally overwhelming his thoughts now, he couldn't think straight, darn it!

He was going to ignore them and he walked quickly towards the trees, back towards his cabin.

"That's the way, that's the way. Quicker, quicker. Hurry, hurry," they were still just as loud as he walked through the trees. Then, they started again, the Ravens, louder and louder they screeched as he hurried through the Forest.

It was driving him crazy all the noise. He could see

small lights appearing at the top of the trees, everywhere they were, and funny musical noises. He could hear the sound of running water too, lots of it, all around him, all directions he could hear rushing water.

The Forest was suddenly all strange to him, he was losing his bearings, hearing things and seeing things, and he needed the toilet again, he needed sleep, he needed... rest.

The Sprites were very happy running here, and flying there, chattering away and were back on their mission to make walkways, lots of little walkways running from tree to tree. Also they were following their orders to annoy the Ravens as much as they could, and they were doing all their jobs very well.

Dino the Dragondoggen did not have the power of flight like your usual dragon because of course he was not a dragon, neither was he a dog nor reptile, just a special blend of them all. He quite liked strolling in the night, as did Freddie Spinner.

This evening they would accompany each other through the Forest, on foot, making quite a bit of noise until the early morning hours. All in the job description of night watchman and guard dog of course.

Tomorrow was the first trial day of sending Scarlett and Mason Beckett back in time. They would exit through the Portal situated with Elvira Vickery and would be entering back (hopefully) through the fields of time-shift on the backs of the two horses, named by Beanie as Celeste and Apollo, the timeless horses.

Everything was in place, the suggestion, the spells and potions, clothing, protection and shoes. If all went well then everything else would be delivered from Marvello the following week.

Their first mission would be to help the orphaned children with no names. No names, no parents, no homes, no hope and a bleak future. This quest would require a great amount of strength, cunning wisdom, courage and sleight of hand trickery.

The Beckett siblings had no idea what lay in store for them the next day. Plenty of others did, a great deal depended on this.

Scarlett lay in bed staring up at the ceiling, thinking. She had a feeling in her waters, a sense of impending doom, a niggling worry, just... something...

CHAPTER EIGHT

The Beckett children arrived at 9 a.m. at No.5 Waters End, home to Elvira. Underneath their old sack clothes and hats they wore the special insoles. The skull rings had taken on a glow about the eyes today. Mason had a few extra bits about his person that may well come in handy, 'Be prepared' was his motto.

Not receiving any answer when they knocked on the door, they made their way around the back of the house where they found Elvira Vickery. "Come in," she said without turning towards them, being far too busy adding little drops of brightly coloured liquid into what appeared to be two very inviting looking milkshakes.

Mixed colours, she offered Scarlett the tall glass with a swirling blue green and mauve mixture, with a creamy looking top and to Mason she gave a slightly smaller glass with red, orange and yellow contents.

"Please bring your drinks and sit." Elvira eyed the pair who did not question her but just sat obediently at the old wooden table and slurped the very tasty mixtures with gusto.

Fruits of Forest, water so pure
Organic herbs and veg for sure
Make us nimble make us quick
Our minds alert tis no trick
The time this day will endless be
But no time will pass for you or me.

Elvira finished reciting her spell and sprinkled dust of purest gold silver and sage all around the two Beckett siblings who were now wide eyed and awaiting their first lesson.

"Now," Elvira began, "we shall start our first history lesson which will focus on 'Witchetty Waters' and how so the islands came to be named. So if you are ready we shall begin, follow me." Elvira walked to the corner of the back room and opened up a wooden trap door set in the heavy stone floor.

"Cool," said Mason. "Another hidden tunnel?"

Elvira smiled at him. "Not quite," she said.

Mr Spangles rubbed himself around their legs as they walked past and he purred, feeling very content today. "*Good luck,*" he said as he sauntered away.

Of course the cat talks too, Scarlett thought as if it were perfectly natural. Mason stuck his thumb up.

Elvira switched on dull lights and they made their way down a few short steps. On the wall was a large white screen, a projector was set up at the back of the room and there were two chairs in the middle. She beckoned Scarlett and Mason to sit on them.

"Sometimes," she said, "it is easier to show you, than to explain with mere words." She switched on the projector and turned off the lights.

In her hand was a long thin stick and she used it as a pointer to highlight everything that was showing in front of them.

"This beats our old school by a million miles," Mason whispered to Scarlett, and she agreed. Where had this old black and white footage come from? It looked so very realistic, she thought.

It was the late 1300s and here was a scene playing from the mainland of Westings, they could see that it was, as the pub The Coach and Horses looked exactly the same as it did now. The Harbour had large galleon ships, these were really old with sails, three sails, flags, oars too and the sides were raised up at each end of the ships. One ship had a very clear name on the side… The Jolly Sea.

There were many people all around the place, dressed the same as Scarlett and Mason and some which were either sailors or pirates wearing black sailors hats or bandanas around their heads. They also had large belts around their waists and across their shoulders. Some had long swords, others had small guns.

A bit further inland there was a small market with a few stalls with wooden tables covered in cloths and bread, vegetables, rolls of cloth, meat and live fish in water buckets were on display.

The roads were cobbled everywhere, some of these cobbled streets still remained. Goats were being traded too. The town buildings were beamed on the outsides. A lot of people mingled outside the pub and when the door opened there were even more on the inside. Mainly these were men sat together at tables looking as thick as thieves, and a lot of business seemed to be going on here.

Children were bedraggled and wandered around the streets. There were very many poor people all over the place, but as usual there was a class divide and the rich also could be seen in much finer clothing.

Elvira Vickery explained that a lot of the population had been wiped out by a plague known as The Black Death, this was first seen in Europe in 1328 and lasted until 1351 although outbreaks had been known after this. Many millions had lost their lives, 200 million in Europe and 35 million Chinese. In comparison it only lasted in England for three years but in that short time had created havoc.

Following this a lot of unrest happened during the reign of King Richard II which led to The Peasants' Revolt in 1381 following the introduction of Poll Tax in 1380. All this happened in the same time that England and France were involved in the 100 year war.

What was not so widely known in the history books was all of the underhand dealings that happened every day. Not only were the common people known as the peasants taxed heavily in England and France, everything taken from them was being stored as bounty, together with treasures taken, looted by pirates, all being guarded under the name of the King.

Nobody would benefit from all this skulduggery that was going on because all of the loot was being stored in tunnels hidden away on the island known as Waters End.

In 1397 the pirates that were the worst bunch on the high seas would go against their direct orders and they undertook to steal everything that had been stored. They planned to sail away for many days and be long gone with all the treasure, as the rumours were rife that the King would one day be overturned. Everything was not as it seemed in the higher classes.

Witchcraft and Magic were showing themselves more and more now, and a lot of this was not known to most of the people. There was indeed a secret society of higher witches and wizards. The members had very specialist powers, potions and spells and they were actually protectors.

They perfected their crafts with the aid of medicinal herbs and wild fruits and found many natural cures for ailments and disease. The modern day ancestors belonging to this blood line were now just three people, Elvira Vickery, Basil Greenleaf and Marvello, none of them were quite what they seemed.

The pirates' luck was soon to run out. No sooner had they loaded up The Jolly Sea ship and set sail, within a very short amount of time the sky had blackened over and a raging storm hit without warning. They stood no chance and the great ship sunk to the depths and all on board went down with her, together with the very precious cargo.

Never had anything like this been seen before, the magnitude was fierce and it was blamed on witchcraft and sorcerers. All those that had been deemed responsible for it were gathered together, all men and women that could not prove their innocence. Many were ordinary folk, but among them were actual wizards and witches of the highest order. They were placed in chains and taken over to the island and left to die in the tunnels.

There they were left, and then the group of islands became known as Witchetty Waters. They did not get visited by any passing ships, afraid that the waters were cursed.

But, they did not die, in fact they were soon free of their binds thanks to their magical powers and the mixture of people which consisted of the mortal, the gifted and Percy Tatterhill's ancestors. They were the guardians of the islands and everything on them until the pirates had overcome them and pillaged all stuff of value. The Tatterhills had not been bound but just left on the island.

It had never been the intention of the Tatterhills to keep any of the ill gotten gains, they oversaw them in the hope one day of turning around all the wrongs and making everything right with the people.

Within months all of the treasures and monies in the chests were retrieved and placed on the six smaller islands bound with spells and such a powerful curse that nobody would ever get to them, except in the passing of time. Only when the time was right that advancement in technology and the true heirs of the islands were in place could the reversal process begin.

King Gregory, ruler of the Realm of the clocks of time and the wise council were now ready, the Beckett family foreseen 600 years before were now in place.

History was about to be re-written. The first History lesson would now continue, not in this classroom in 2016 but back on the cobbled streets of Westings in the year 1377, the year King Richard II took the throne.

Elvira had placed medic bags and supplies of food and drink into two small leather bags which she gave to Scarlett and Mason.

"Now," she said to them, "you will be going on a little journey to finish your lesson, make your way through the town and keep going uphill. It would be wise to stay together, keep your heads down and what you will be looking out for at the top of the hill are two horses, you will know them, you have seen them on this island."

"Which way do we go?" asked Scarlett.

"Through here," said Elvira, waving a wand in

circular motions which opened up a Portal that the two children entered into and disappeared.

Meanwhile back deep in the forest Septimus has started to go stir crazy. He had locked himself in a small cupboard in the middle of the night and had not had more than an hour's sleep in the last 48 hours.

It started late last evening just as he had dropped off to sleep exhausted from the day and night before. He heard a really loud whooshing sound outside the door followed by loud bangs all around the cabin, he had jumped out of bed, opened the door, and there was nothing? Not a thing.

He got back into bed and pulled the covers over his head grunting and cursing, his tired eyes shutting once more, he dropped off to sleep. Moments later he was awoken again by loud banging on the windows, bang, bang, bang.

He jumped up again, tripped over his blankets and landed in a heap on the floor, banging his head on the way down. He was really annoyed now. "Who the blinking heck is that?" he shouted, finding his feet and heading towards the window. He threw it open.

"Good evening," said Dino deliberately belching out the smell of his very fishy supper. *"Just checking the area for snakes, mice, frogs and such like, did I wake you?"*

What on earth Septimus was looking at he had no idea, a talking stinking beast of a thing right here at his cabin. It wasn't right, he knew that.

"Be gone with ya," Septimus snarled, although he felt himself shaking. Dino whipped up his long strong tail and banged the window shut with great ferocity and shifted from view.

"My turn next," grinned Freddie.

They waited half an hour and Freddie turned on powerful floodlights that had been set up high on the trees and directed straight at the log cabin, lighting up the whole area so brightly it was like daylight. Freddie then started up a chainsaw and proceeded to start cutting a large tree standing right next to the cabin.

Septimus stumbled out of bed and opened the door. He immediately shielded his eyes from the intense light, it was blinding him.

Freddie stopped the saw, and shouted to Septimus, "It's alright, don't be alarmed, just following orders to remove six large trees tonight from immediately around this cabin." Septimus knew that voice, it was that Davy man.

"Is that you Dingle?" he shouted out.

"Not me," said Freddie. "Tommy Tinderbox the tree surgeon, that's me."

Dino swept past Septimus and caught him swiftly with his tail, bringing him to his knees. *"How clumsy of me."*

The sawing noise carried on for three more hours, it was the middle of the night, then it stopped. The Sprites once again resumed their activity making more racket than ever before. The Ravens stirred up, screeching and swirling around, stooping down and screeching louder. The sprites dropped nuts, hundreds of them inside the log cabin chimney.

Enough, enough," yelled Septimus, his head was thumping with all the noise. He scooped up his blankets and got into his cupboard. He locked the door, and that's where he stayed, not sleeping, just crouched down, huddled.

The break of day bought a silence with it and Septimus strained his ears to see if it had all finally stopped. He unlocked the cupboard door and went into the kitchen, but it was dark, very dark, because outside it was piled up with logs. He opened the door and outside that too was piled up with logs, he couldn't get out.

Not sure if he could trust his mind anymore he panicked and made his way to the centre of the room feeling around the furniture. Pulling the large chair away, he lifted up the wooden door to his secret tunnel and got inside it.

He felt up on the ledge for matches and lit the torch he kept there. Just barely able to see, he slowly walked along the bumpy floor. This tunnel hadn't been used for years, it led to one place he did not want to go right now, the hidden bay cave, for his company there would be hundreds of bats, and dead pirates.

He needed to get away from this place and the strange creatures and goings on that were sending his mind crazy. Nobody would find him there he thought, that would be another mistake on his part.

"*He is going through the tunnel hee hee hee,*" one of the head fairies called out as she swept up out of the chimney and flew around Freddie Spinner's head.

"Come Dino boy," shouted out Freddie and Dino bounded over towards the cabin and proceeded to knock away the piles of logs with his enormous strong tail. "I shall go and fetch Tom Beckett now and old Ted Bakewell, we will make short work of taking this cabin to pieces," he winked.

They surely did, by ten o'clock that morning nothing was left standing, and there was an enormous lorry load of wood ready to take away.

Also taken apart was the shed with bolt croppers, a very handy tail and three pairs of hands. Everything inside was transported over to an outside storage shed of Tom's. From now on he would be taking on the role of wood cutter along with his other duties.

The entrance to the hidden tunnel was now covered, concealed by an old tractor which would stay there for the time being.

"Nice day to go fishing," Ted said. "I may well go a little further out today, all around the island in actual fact," he laughed.

"Beware of the ghosts," warned Tom as he walked off shaking his head. *Ghosts!* he thought, *Pirate ghosts? I'll believe it when I see it.*

Grace was pleased to have the house to herself this morning and the fact that they were due a visitor to connect them to the world wide web at last. Not your usual provider, in fact Percy had told her it would be all done in the blink of an eye and the drop of a hat. A cordless phone and a fancy little box.

Making herself a coffee she wondered how Scarlett and Mason's day was going.

CHAPTER NINE

Scarlett and Mason felt themselves being swirled around and lifted up into a swirly mist of colours and then they zoomed backwards at a speed you could not even imagine and everything whirled passed them in a crazy haze.

Then it stopped and they fell backwards out of the mist and landed on a hard mud floor inside a deep dark cave.

"That," said Mason, "was the most mind blowing thing in the world, ever."

"It was like being on the world's fastest Roller Coaster, without the bends and a million times faster," gasped Scarlett.

"Any idea where we are?" Mason asked. He took out his Compass which at this moment was just spinning around endlessly. "Curious." He had a torch which he flicked on and shone around them.

"Some sort of a cave, we need to try and find our way out of here," replied Scarlett.

They stood and steadied themselves trying to get their bearings. "I feel a draught of air, come on this way," said Mason and he shone the torch out in front of them.

Scarlett was happy to follow, after all this was her brother's forte, survival games! They slowly made their way to what was hopefully the entrance of this dark cavern.

The sound of water could be heard dripping around them from the roof. Mason shone the torch above them and stopped. "Look up there Sis." She did so and shuddered at the sight of the bats just hanging upside down, loads of them.

"Let's hurry up and get out of here," she whispered, worried that they would fly at them and dreading to think what else could be lurking around in this dark dank place.

They were being watched from a dark corner of the cave by a man standing silently, he was dressed in black robes and hood. All you could see were the whites of his eyes. He had waited a long time for this moment to come.

He tapped his long wooden cane sharply on the cavern floor three times. The Beckett children stopped in their tracks and looked fearfully at each other.

"Stay where you are." The figure slowly emerged from the darkness and stealthily walked towards them. "The children from the future, you have arrived safely, and indeed proved that there is no doubt you are the two chosen ones." Innocent of heart, but fearless, he thought.

Scarlett looked at this very tall man that had suddenly appeared before them. "Who are you?" she asked nervously and put a protective arm around her little brother.

"I," came the reply, "am Druleus, Keeper of Secrets, and Head Wizard of the higher wizards and witches of middle age times. At this moment in time too, your protector. How much have you been told by Elvira as to why you are here?" Druleus enquired with one eyebrow raised up.

"We were in the middle of a History lesson and then... boom... we were sort of transported here to finish it," Mason said this as he was busy glancing over this Druleus person, who it seemed to him was at least seven foot tall and a lot more mysterious than Marvello.

"To be precise," added Scarlett, "we were shown a film of Westings and told of the great storm of 1397 that sunk The Jolly Sea Ship and all on board, a witches' curse, a crooked King called Richard the II and some peasants revolting. Basically," she added as an afterthought.

"Do you know what year this is?" Druleus asked them.

"Of course, it's 2016, anyone knows that," said Mason.

Druleus gave a wry smile. "Not quite my boy. At the end of this day for you then it shall be 2016 if all goes to plan, but as it happens, the year at this moment is 1377 and some things you have spoken of have yet to pass."

"1377?" they both shouted at once. "1377?"

"But how, what do you mean, 1377?" Scarlett looked at this Sorcerer type giant with her hands on her hips wanting many answers.

Had they not been under so much influence with the suggestive scones it would probably have been a total freak out time in their lives!

"Come with me my children, there is still clearly a lot to explain."

Druleus spun around holding onto his very heavy robe, and wand in hand he swirled into the air quickly creating a bright light centred onto the cavern wall. Once again a film appeared similar to what they had been watching not long ago at No. 5 Waters End with Elvira Vickery.

So, their lesson continued: *Richard the II has just been crowned King and a lot will happen over the next 23 years until his disappearance in 1399 and 'death' in 1400 whilst the people are under his reign.*

Times are very hard both in England and in France, and the people suffer too much, it was not written into History that such poverty and suffering would take place. Fate will need a hand to get it back on the right path and change the course of the future for all.

To make the world a much better place as a result, we need to start here on the Kentish Coast.

The domino effect will stop poverty across England and Europe in the generations to come. The first change that needs to be made will be to stop the suffering of the children and so a sanctuary will be built on the Second Island for the orphans and their 'carers'.

To do this many changes will be made, through trickery and foresight which is where you both come into the picture.

There are many quests that you will need to conquer. Rebalancing the flow of fortunes.

Remember, that one day these islands will be owned by your family. Yes, if all goes as it should and history is re-written one day the islands will be known as 'The Becketts Havens'.

"Aren't we a bit young to be a pair of heroes?" asked Scarlett. "This sounds like a massive tall order."

"I don't mind being a hero," said Mason. "Not one little bit."

"You will not be heroes today," smiled Druleus. "This is an experiment to see if you could get here through the portal of time safely and then get back to your own time through the time shift fields on the backs of the two timeless horses that travel without effort. The return journey will be a lot smoother.

"Scarlett, you have been chosen by fate for these tasks which have been set by The Wise Council of King Gregory ruler of *The Realm of the clocks of time*. This was meant to be, it's your calling.

"Between the two of you the knowledge of wisdom and sleight of hand will be enough, together with many aids that will be shortly given to you by Marvello.

"The very powerful rings of protection that you both now wear gifted by Sophia Bonetti, which I may add were delivered to her shop *Contessa Alessa* by the very same time owls residing in your barn, and the spells from here there and everywhere will ensure your safety.

"We hope," he added quietly.

"Do you remember what you were told to do

today?" asked Druleus.

"Yes, to make our way up the hill towards the horses," replied Mason.

"Good, then off you both go."

With that the tall wizard walked towards the wall from where he came and he vanished.

Mason once again put his torch back on and they carried on silently toward the cold air and the light at the end of the cavern.

Outside there were trees all around one side and they realised that they were above the town already but not quite at the top of the hill. Mason looked at his compass and it had now returned to normal. Facing upward it showed him that it was a South Westerly direction.

They decided not to take advantage of their super fast shoes as they weren't sure of the exact location just yet that they needed to be.

It looked pretty surreal down in the harbour with the old Galleon ships, not at all like it normally would be with the fishing boats and ferries.

"What do you make of all this then Mason, do you think we can really do whatever it is they are expecting of us?"

Before he could answer, a small boy came out from behind the bushes and eyed them both with alarm, not expecting them to be there. This child looked cold, hungry and frightened. Mason reached into his bag and held out some biscuits for him. The boy grabbed them and after smelling them, greedily stuffed them into his mouth and ran away.

"Course we can, we *have* to." Her smaller brother looked for the first time as if he was starting to be a bit more grown up, and thoughtful.

Keeping to the edge of the trees they made their way uphill. "What if we can't get back?" Scarlett asked, genuinely scared.

"Of course we will," Mason smiled. Shut up, he thought.

After about fifteen minutes the trees ended and all that was left were fields. They were almost at the top of the hill and in the distance the shape of the two horses were visible.

Without cover now they both decided it would be best to run like the wind with the help of their insoles, so they did.

A couple of minutes later they skidded to a halt having arrived just where they were meant to. "Fingers crossed," said Mason. The horses came down onto their front legs and Scarlett climbed onto the smaller one, the beautiful Dapple Grey and Mason jumped onto the large Black Stallion.

Neither horse had reins or a saddle but each had two small handles made of thick twine either side of their necks that just grew from the inside out.

A glowing mist appeared around them and they felt themselves shoot forwards and upwards at such a speed that sparks flew all around them, and within seconds they descended softly onto the grassy fields.

The horses galloped forward and made their way downhill slowing down to a canter and then a trot.

Scarlett's hair was all over her face, she brushed it

aside and peered forwards. She could make out their house at No. 1 Waters End in the distance and the barn and sheds and forest. "Yes," she laughed out loud. "We're home again."

The horses stopped still and bent down for the brother and sister to dismount. Then they turned and galloped off into the distance.

"Let's sit for a minute," Mason said. They both sat down onto the grass. "So, just to be sure, we have to go back there again and basically save the world, or thereabouts, is that right?"

Scarlett pondered for a minute. "That just about sums it up, not save the world exactly, but create an alternative one, maybe."

"Do you think Mum and Dad know about any of this?" Mason asked again.

"I'm not sure of anything anymore, just look what's happened the past few weeks," Scarlett said. "In a nutshell we have left an ordinary boring life, come to an island that takes us back in time with a talking Dragon/dog for a pet, a supernatural cat belonging to a witch, and all sorts of trickery everywhere."

Goblins, Fairies, Elves, Sand Duners, Runners and ghostly pirates were as yet to be introduced to them. It was all about to get a lot more tricky.

Above all of this was an alien life form bubbling away in the very deep waters surrounding them and if Mason had any idea about that, any at all, he would have thought all of his Christmases had come at once.

Only one person was aware of this, King Gregory

of *The Realm of the clocks of time*. He was the only person that knew everything that went on, in whichever domain, at any time.

Mr Spangles flew over the trees. He had been patiently waiting on the forest's edge for the safe arrival of their two saviours heading home on horseback. He was now very pleased to be going to report back to Elvira that the experiment had been a success.

The two of them pulled the sack clothing over their heads and walked home in their normal clothing as if it had just been another day at school.

"We're back," shouted out Mason slamming the front door behind them. Scarlett hung her bag up on the hook and they walked toward the large front room with the log fire burning and slumped into two easy chairs.

What was this?

A black upright phone was situated in the corner along with a black box that glowed all around the edges with a gold light, situated (because that's what it was) in mid-air, suspended. Mason walked over to it and run his hand underneath it... nothing... he tried above it... nothing... and then he swirled both arms all around it... nothing.

Almost immediately the phone started to ring, a most fascinating ring tone, not one that either of them had heard anywhere before. It sounded more like bells ringing.

Mason snatched at the phone and pressed the gold flashing display. "Hello," he said, desperate to know who had this number, he certainly didn't.

"To whom am I speaking?" asked the voice on the other end.

"Mason Beckett here," Mason replied.

"Ah good, I see the line is working perfectly well. Please dial code 01231 plus the number in the black book for Mr Tatterhill or anybody else on the mainland... 05 for Miss Elvira Vickery, 03 for Beanie, 07 for Basil Greenleaf and it's 08 for the Village Store, your number of course is 01. Is there anything else I can do for you today?"

"No I don't think so," replied Mason.

"Thank you for choosing *Magic Airwaves* as your provider." The phone went silent.

Mason let go of it and it remained suspended. Almost immediately one long beep was heard and the phone automatically went into an answering mode. *'Miss Vickery here, it's Geography tomorrow, comfortable clothing will do, please find your new school bags in your rooms together with your lists, good afternoon to you both.'*

On the bureau there was now a beautiful black leather bound telephone & address book embossed with gold writing, which Scarlett opened and flicked through the pages.

Neatly written on every page was everybody they had ever known, all friends and family plus every single number for all of the buildings in Westings, including the pub.

She placed it back down and they headed to the kitchen, something smelled good and they were both starving.

Their Mother turned to greet them. "I have been

making a few special treats for tea tonight," she said, "I expect you are both ravenous after your first day back, how was it?"

"It was very… interesting," Scarlett smiled.

Mason nodded in agreement, "Great teacher, nowhere near as boring as our old school, can't wait for tomorrow."

"Are you feeling alright dear?" his mother laughed. Grace was happy it went so well. "As you've probably seen, the phone line is up and running and the internet. Strange little man, wasn't here more than a moment, a new suspension kit or something, isn't it wonderful?"

She carried over two plates brimming with rainbow coloured chips and red burgers with blue onion rings. "New recipes, speciality to the island apparently." She held up *'Island Speciality Cook Book Volume 1'*.

"Oh yes a large parcel arrived for you both, special school supplies from *Confusion Illusion.*"

CHAPTER TEN

Freddie Spinner was now no longer Night watchman but was instead put on a permanent payroll. Together with Beanie, Basil, Tom and Ted, the team of men were turning the storage facility into something more spacious.

A new home for Freddie, with the aid of a lorry load of logs and roofing dismantled from the forest former residence of Septimus Dread.

"Did you see anything yesterday out on your boat?" Tom Beckett asked Ted.

Ted gave him a knowing glance, "Can't say that I did, strange that. I moored up around the other side of the island, had a stroll inside the cave and all round about, nothing, didn't see him anywhere." Ted was rather puzzled.

"I saw him," Freddie piped up.

"Where did you see him?" asked Beanie.

"Who me?" Freddie pointed to himself. "Dunno

what you're talking about, I never seen no-one."

He was going to be hard work, thought Tom, smiling to himself.

"By the way Tom, I have a little something for your Mason," Beanie said.

"Oh yes, what's that then?"

"Well, when I say a little something, it's a few little somethings, rabbits!"

"I had a rabbit once," said Freddie.

"Did you?" replied Beanie.

"No, I didn't," said Freddie and he carried on banging wood together.

"What was that?" Ted said as they all looked up when a rushing wind swept past them at great speed then disappeared.

"Darned if I know," said Tom.

"I know what it is," said Freddie.

"What?" said Beanie.

"Got no idea," said Freddie.

Scarlett and Mason had just passed them on their way to No. 5 and lesson number two, Geography. It was quite ridiculous, Scarlett had thought, bags no bigger than 7 inches by 5 inches and they were crammed full with their lists of items plus the essentials that Mason insisted on packing.

They now contained gloves, ear phones, eye patches, knee pads, pens, pencils, paper, a complete picnic as they would be out all day today, a walkie talkie each, raincoats (just in case) and Wellington boots.

The bags were bottomless pits so to speak, they did not fill up and they weighed nothing at all hanging across their bodies.

Mason thought this was the coolest thing ever, of course his contained everything from Marvello's shop his Dad had bought him, and half of his bedroom... basically.

When they skidded to a stop at Elvira Vickery's house, they found her outside waiting for them. "Good morning to you both, I would like to give you this," and she handed over a small electronic gadget, it was black with a gold display.

"A geography lesson with a twist," she swirled her wand around the device and it pinged into life. "This is your wayfinder," she explained. "To test your knowledge and skills. You will be going alone today, your objective is to find the spot marked with an X."

She placed her finger across her lips indicating for them not to speak.

"You have been loaded with 100 points inside the wayfinder, use it well. To ask questions you will lose points, to become lost you will also lose points, to go under 50 points on your return means your choices in geography were not wise ones and you will fail the test."

When Elvira said they would be going alone, it was not quite strictly true, as the wily foxes could be found wandering the forest. They were very sly creatures. The sand duners which could be troublesome little hinderers, and the hundreds of fruit bats could scare them off of course.

She had taken little precautions to balance up the

odds a bit.

Mr Spangles was already in flight and would have them in his radar, also the barn owls were trained to fly to Beanie as a silent gesture that he was needed.

Dino the Dragondoggen was also freely wandering around the island today, should his 'skills' be required at all.

She wanted to see what the pair were really capable of on the darker side of the island, and with just their senses to guide them.

Everybody was occupied, including Mrs Bakewell, again going over to visit Grace Beckett with more recipes and chat. All seemed to be going to plan at the moment.

Just one fly in the ointment, where on Earth had Septimus Dread disappeared too? He was last seen fumbling through a tunnel which led to the hidden bat cave.

Elvira had glanced into her crystal ball but even with its scanning mists she had not spotted him. Although not a bright man he was a determined one, *and* he was on the loose.

She rang Percy and informed him of the latest developments and her concern for the missing Woodman. By now he should have been safely off the island.

Percy was of mixed emotions, very elated, very elated indeed that Scarlett and Mason had been back and forth in time, unharmed and were now being prepared with special 'training'. This had been overshadowed by the disappearance of one who was not going to leave quietly… at least not while his mission for vast treasures was still in his mind. What to do?

Septimus Dread did not have a very good time of it going from one end of the tunnel to the other and nor did he when he got to the other end, and into the hidden bat cave.

"Shiver me timbers."

"Pieces of eight."

"In the riggin."

"Thar she blows."

"Ahoy there."

All around him were the ghostly pirates darting around the cave walls, shooting straight through him. He put his hands up across his face and hurried past them and outside.

Ain't nobody going to give me any peace, his mind was racing, he was muttering away to himself, seeing things that weren't there, things that were there, things in between and much more besides.

There was only one place to go he knew, a place where he could rest undisturbed, the final resting place of his Uncle. An underground tomb.

Only he knew where it was. He had dug it out himself and had spent the odd night there before, 'talking' to the old lumberjack, not getting any answers mind, just talking.

That's where he went, and that's where he had stayed until two hours ago. He had then made his way back through the cave and the tunnel back to his cabin. When he got there of course he couldn't get out, try as he might, the old trapdoor wouldn't budge an inch. Something was wrongly afoot about this place.

It was then he decided that he didn't think he was welcome on this island anymore. Well, blow them all and damn them, he thought. He had a few tricks up his sleeve, he could stay fed watered and sheltered, they weren't going to get rid of him that easily. He knew their game, at least now he could spend even more time treasure hunting. He would find it, even if it killed him.

His only option at this moment was to go back the way he had come, back to the other side of the island once more.

Scarlett had been spending a lot of her spare time reading through the library books and in her head she was quite familiar with the rough layout of the direction they were headed. Mostly they walked, keeping an eye on the wayfinder to make sure the cross was still in view.

"I think," she said to Mason, "that we are heading towards a place that is known as the Hidden Bay, and from what I know about that, it's large, full of bats and was used as a dropping off point by pirates. A base where treasure was transported by tunnels and hidden around the island, also chests full of money that was taken from the peasants."

"Sounds like a nice place!" Mason said.

"Oh it gets better, apparently it is also haunted by the ghost pirates that went down with The Jolly Sea ship, that's also deep under the water around that side too," Scarlett told him.

"Dunno about a geography lesson, more like a spooky one. Sounds great, can't wait to see this." Mason actually felt quite excited.

"You can see the next island from around there too, it's not that far really, maybe we can get to go to it one day in the other little boat?" Scarlett carried on explaining the layout of the land around all the island that she had researched from their old house and read up on over the last few days.

Mason was half listening to the rest of it, concentrating on the direction they were headed and wondering exactly what it was that all these new 'gadgets' did that had been delivered.

"Let's stop a few minutes," he said. "We need to check some stuff out." They sat themselves down on some large rocks and he delved into his bag.

"Ok, let's see what these do." Firstly, he took out the eye patch and placed it over his eye. "Oh my goodness," he shouted. "Quick Scarlett, get your one out." She did so and put hers on as well.

"Oh my giddy Aunt," she said.

They both sat still and were amazed that they could see everything all around their heads, the whole complete circle. "360 degree vision," said Mason.

"Yes, and look ahead of you," said Scarlett, they could both now see a whole lot further than they could before.

"Wicked," Mason took his off and pulled out the earphones. Everything was so amplified, he could hear the men talking back on the beach and they were way over an hour away from them. Scarlett again copied her brother, she could hear something odd as well.

"Listen to that," she pointed down to the sand.

"*This way, this way, hurry, hurry, come on, come on, move it, move it.*" They were not alone on the beach, something was under the sand, many somethings by the sound of it, what on Earth could it be?

Of course trailing their every move were the sand duners. Both nosey and naughty.

Scarlett dug deep into her bag and pulled out the last two items delivered yesterday.

Thin gloves, she tried these on and nothing seemed to happen. "I wonder what these are for?" she asked Mason. He put his on as well and pointed with them, nothing happened. He rubbed his hands together and whoosh, a bright light shone out. He placed his hands down near the ground in between the rocks where the light was even brighter.

"Amazing, our own torchlights, wicked!"

And lastly they took out their kneepads and fastened them on. "I don't think they are to help us walk quicker or anything, our insoles do that trick." Mason thought for a moment and then got down onto his knees in the sand, he pressed down on his knees and shot up into the air.

"Woah," he laughed, "you gotta try these babies." Him and Scarlett spent the next five minutes trying out the pads on different surfaces seeing who could get the highest. They were getting almost as high up as the trees, the harder the surface, the more 'bounce' they got.

"Stop, stop," she shouted to him. "We have to get on with what we were doing." It was so exhilarating everything that they had been given. They had been side-tracked.

They carried on walking again. "The thing is Mason, all of this might be a lot of fun, but we have been given all of this for a reason, and we have to work that out."

After a few minutes he replied, "So, we can see a lot and hear a lot and have the power to run away at great speed or spring really high upwards and light up the darkest places on the planet."

"Exactly," she answered. "Do you get the feeling we will need all the help we can get? I think this will be a lot harder than we first thought, whatever it is that we have to do. We got some catching up to do," she said. "Fancy a run?"

Elvira gave a quick push of a button on her screen to see whereabouts the pair were. Halfway there and still on course, good, time for a test, she thought.

Moon and Sun be Sun and Moon
Let midnight take the place of noon
Stars awake and shineth bright
Tis now your world the dark of night

Scarlett and Mason stopped abruptly, what was going on now? One minute it was daytime and now it was the pitch black night. The moon shone brightly and the clear night sky was full of stars.

Mason looked very puzzled, as did Scarlett, the wayfinder was now on a night mode screen and the X marking the spot was illuminated. They were heading in the same direction but they couldn't see. "Find your gloves," Scarlett said.

"Think we need our eye patches too," Mason suggested.

"Let's just keep all our equipment on, never know what we will need," said Scarlett. Up above them was just a pair of cat's eyes flying around in the dark, the rest of the body unseen.

The light from the gloves was truly bright, like headlights on full beam. They carried on walking. They could hear the voices under the sand again following them along, they needed to change course slightly and they headed towards the forest.

"I have never seen anywhere so dark," whispered Scarlett. "Imagine if we never had this light at our hands, it would be like a power cut everywhere."

"Yes, just like in old times don't you think?" Mason said. "I get it, we are being tested because back in time where we have to go there was no electricity the world would be this... this black."

"Clever boy," said Scarlett. "Of course and we will have to find our way in the dark sometimes."

"Now we have got to reach our destination in the pitch black, using our instincts. Good job I have skills," Mason bragged. "No matter what time we're in, if it's dark then we can let the North star guide our way. We need to brush up on the compass points for everywhere on this island, and on the mainland too." He was leaving little markers upon the trees as they went.

If she were being honest, this was not her favourite past-time, being in the woods in the middle of the night. But she was the eldest if not the bravest, so she focused her mind again on the geography of the islands and she was sure that she could hear water running this time around, which she couldn't locate last time.

She would be correct of course because now the forest did indeed have running water that was making its way across the darker side of the island too.

"The stream," she said to Mason. "If we can find it then it runs adjacent to the sea which means we just follow it and it should lead us all the way to the hidden bay where the inlet of water starts."

No need for walkie talkies anymore, they could see all around, hear for miles and light up brightly everything around them, but still, it would be up to their choices, not gadgets.

So, everything was lit up brightly with the glove torches, they could see everything around them literally and with their new heightened hearing they made themselves head towards the direction of the water. It was very helpful, just like having most of their senses heightened plus some extra powers chucked in.

The Ravens started their screeching and flew high over the trees, totally thrown off course. One part of the sky was day, another small part was night, and where was the man that had lived in the woods, and the house that they flew to each night? They flew around bewildered and squawking.

Very soon afterwards, the pair found the stream

and the water in it was the purest they had ever seen. They carried on walking against the flow of the water and would stay on this path until they found the source. Convinced that it would be the location of the bay and the inlet from the sea.

"Listen," said Scarlett. "Do you hear something?" Mason stopped walking, he could hear a funny small high pitched voice.

"Yes," he said and looked upwards, high up in the trees were small glowing lights that danced around.

"Shall we take a look up there, see what it is?" he asked his Sister.

"I think we should," she said and they both bent down onto their knees. "On the count of three," Scarlett said and they pushed down on the knee pads one, two, three times and leapt straight up.

Grabbing at the branches as they shot up high into the air they found themselves face to face with some strange little beings.

The Sprites were flying and running about everywhere. Little walkways from branches to branches were swinging wildly as the siblings had just disturbed them. There was a whole kingdom of little people up here, fairies, elves and goblins. What on Earth?

A small fairy who had the brightest of all the wings flew down in front of their faces. "*Hello,*" she said, "*my name is Caelia, and I am the Queen of the Fairies.*"

This little creature glowed, her very bright hair in a small golden bun held up with small twigs and flowers and her dress was purest white.

Some more little fairies came into view and fluttered their wings all around them. Trixie, Fae, Una, Idalis, Tertia all gave their names. Each one equally enchanting and their small dresses were yellow, green, pink, mauve and blue.

"We are Scarlett and Mason Beckett," Scarlett explained, not quite sure how to address these little creatures that up until now she had believed were just mythical.

"On our way to the Hidden Bat Cave, on an important mission," added Mason. "Are we headed in the right direction?" he asked. How strange is this, he was thinking. With that the wayfinder pinged and on the display it said in large gold writing, points 90. "Ooops, shouldn't have asked that," he frowned. He would be careful not to make that mistake again.

The fairies all laughed together. "*The trials are yours alone, we have been sent here to rid the forest of Septimus Dread and restore all the dark places to their natural beauty once again,*" Caelia explained kindly.

Mason was about to ask who sent them and decided better of it, just in case.

"*I am Bottleaxe and this is my husband Dipstix,*" bellowed out a small, green, long eared Goblin. They wore matching war robes draped over one shoulder, carrying small shields and little stick knives.

Scarlett wanted to laugh but instead bit her lip and turned her head away. "*And these,*" belted out the feisty female Goblin, "*are Foghorn, Dimmerwit, Bancheesie and Gibberish.*"

"*At your service,*" Foghorn bellowed. Large lungs for little fellows these Goblin types. There were many more Fairies and Goblins going about their business.

"There is an easier way down for you," Caelia pointed towards an opening in the tree trunk. *"The tree elves have carved out the insides, you should fit. There are snacks, help yourself to any and remember that all flowing water in the forests are now as pure as the rain, quite drinkable."*

She flew away leaving a trail of light behind her. The inside of the tree was huge and nothing like you would imagine it to be from the outside. They made their way down the centre which was totally taken away, carefully placing their hands and feet on the edges where little spiral steps were carved for the small folk, with stores of nuts and berries everywhere.

They quickly reached the bottom where there was a hinged doorway. They pushed it open and crawled through, being a little bit large for it. There stood outside was a tree elf dressed in red busily sanding off a small mushroom stool that had been shaped out of the tree innards.

"Edwig Barkski, furniture maker and Elf extraordinaire, that's me." This creature stood larger than the others, at all of 8-10 inches tall.

Such a busy area nobody took the time to stop and entertain the Becketts further, they were all far too busy. So, with introductions over they carried on along the edge of the stream. A little further along it forked off to the right where the stream continued and to the left was a beautiful waterfall, this they would leave for the next time.

And as soon as they had found the stream it just as abruptly ended. The water was still flowing towards them but it was blocked, just as the trees overhead were darker and clumped together. It would seem that the sprites were making their way backwards from the inhabited side of the island to the empty part. Working and transforming the forest.

"Nothing else for it, we will have to either try and make our way through this thick bramble and undergrowth with no real sense of direction or turn right back towards the beach and follow the water's edge all around to get there," Scarlett said, they decided that would be a much better option.

It would not even be possible to jump up with the pads, it was far too dense. Using their bright glove hands and the compass and the night sky high above, they tried their best to work their way out again.

Again Mason left markers in the trees, pins with white cloth attached if they needed to retrace their steps.

They were on the right track. Mr Spangles could see they would soon be out of the forest, which was just as well, the sly foxes had been tailing them and pulling out with their teeth all of the markers which had been left behind.

Once more they found the sand under their feet and made their way to the water's edge. It was time to get a spurt on so once again and with a very clear vision in front of them, they used the advantage of speed, around 70mph speed to make up lost time and sped towards the bend leading to the cave.

With the air whooshing past them, and free of all obstacles they finally made it to the spot marked X. Seeing an entrance ahead of them, they quickly skidded to a halt, kicking sand up everywhere.

And, as suddenly as night had befallen them, it turned back into day, the bright winter sun shining a dim light into the trees.

They rubbed their hands together turning the bright light off. Just at that moment and before they removed their earphones, they both heard voices coming from inside the cave.

"Shiver me timbers, walk the plank, ho ho ho and a bottle of rum."

"What the heck was that?" Mason whispered, looking at Scarlett.

Something else was in that cave too, apart from the squeaking noises of bats there was a grunting.

"Damn them all, pesky family, I'll show them," and a bit more muttering besides, it was getting louder. They ducked down behind a large rock, and then out came the mad axeman from the woods, swearing and a cursing to himself. He disappeared into the trees nearby, then he went silent.

They stood and crept towards the entrance to the cave. *"Pieces of eight me hearties."* Mason rubbed his hands together and out shone the bright light, it all fell silent, completely silent.

"You have reached your destination," the wayfinder called out, making them both jump.

CHAPTER ELEVEN

"Message alert," the wayfinder beeped out. Scarlett opened the message, *"Congratulations for finding the spot marked X but your geography lesson does not end here, you will now find your way across to island number two, and remember the rules, you have 40 points left or you will fail this test, good luck."*

A new spot marked X appeared on the screen together with 90 points across the top. They left the hidden cave and took a moment outside to think the next part through. Less than fifty points was a fail.

Scarlett and Mason removed their gloves and both noticed how the eyes of their skull rings were glowing brightly. The rings of protection were on high alert right now.

"Well it's too far to jump to!" Mason quipped.

"As yet we have no powers to fly," Scarlett smirked. "So… we have two choices, A we swim or B we go back and get a boat from the moorings." At least she knew that island number two was the closest to them and the second largest island in the group.

"As it's almost winter, that's a no brainer," Mason said, not at all sure he could swim quite that far anyway. So once again the power of their insoles got them back to the small harbour in no time at all and they untied the smaller of the boats meaning they just had oar power and slowly set themselves off around the island once more.

It was hard work even though the sea was very calm today so they took it in turns. "What we could do with is super fast arm power wristbands to complete our set up," Scarlett sighed. That gave Mason a thought, maybe he could mix up a potion with ingredients from Marvello's, he thought. After all they did have wristbands already, an even quicker arm and hand movement would be even better for tricking people too.

Elvira resisted the urge to summon the slinky seals to help them along, after all they had lessons to learn and quickly. Tomorrow they would be going back to 1377 Westings Mainland, and this time they had a task to complete.

Dino had sniffed him out, he had found the spot where Septimus was lurking around in the tomb of his Uncle. Using his nose, he circled all around the area to where the scent had stopped and he lay himself down. He would wait for him to come back out of wherever he was hiding. The trail stopped here.

Mr Spangles glided gracefully through the air, he wanted to arrive at the second island before the Beckett siblings did. It would not be hard as their speed had slowed right down, they were actually using this time in the boat for their picnic lunch, taking it in turns with the oars.

What a lunch it was too. Bread rolls with multi coloured stripes of red and yellow seeds on top filled with bright pink tuna, herby topping and special seafood sauce, green. Banana and Oatmeal biscuits, a delicate shade of purple and milkshakes, surprisingly cold still laid with gold bronze and silver stars mingled with plain vanilla ice-cream and yellow strawberry topping.

Basil Greenleaf stood watching through his binoculars at the two small figures in the boat. Getting a bit more than their five a day there, he thought to himself. Everything they were now consuming contained powerful immune system boosters and plenty of stamina. They would soon have super human strength on this diet, they would need it.

Neither of them knew as they were idling away in the small boat what they had just passed over. Deep in the depths of the ocean where everything was totally black concealed at the back of an alcove was a box, a box that was glowing and beeping green in time with its Mother ship, hidden away and slowly creating alien life.

One box had already been dropped back in 1397, taking hundreds of years to alter the environment around it, and this was the second part of the evolving life cycle now ready to incubate in the adapted water. Part of a big plan from another species in faraway Andromeda Galaxy to inhabit this Planet that man was slowly destroying. A very evolved species that used a craft to time travel in space as they had broken the speed of light.

King Gregory, ruler of *The Realm of the clocks of time* was now in a race to alter the course of history to stop this happening. The sea needed someone 600 years ago to discover what was lurking deep. A reason to be at the depths. The clock was ticking, so to speak.

An hour and a bit later the pair were crossing from the point of the hidden bay and had almost reached island number two.

The Runners had been gathered by Mr Spangles. They were ordered to stop their running and assemble at meeting point number one. Their feet were twitching, they found it very hard to keep still, but keep still they would, and here they would stay until the visitors had left the island today.

At last they arrived, the part of the journey from one island to another had been a little bit rocky in the water. No harbour anywhere here so Scarlett took off her trainers and socks, rolled her trouser legs up and standing in the shallow water, pulled the small boat to shore. Quite easily in fact, she was getting quite fit lately.

Mason jumped out onto the sand and helped her pull the boat out of the water where they found a wooden sea defence and tied the boat to it.

Although they were on the island, the wayfinder still had the second X spot a bit of a distance away. They made their way towards the thick trees.

It was very quiet here, no obvious signs of life. Very eerie compared to Waters End, which although remote was inhabited and seemed like a large town compared to this.

No doubt there was a fair bit of wildlife here just the same. They stopped, just ahead of them was what looked like a signpost but there was something attached to it. Mason walked ahead and grabbed it, a small black gadget similar to their wayfinder but magnetic on the back. He turned the power button on and the screen shot to life with a message box to open.

Travel back to times gone by
Seek the boy known then as Si
Your magic tricks will make him see
That just like you he too can be
Find the girl with raven hair
Fira lives in hidden lair
Give her knowledge of this day
Together you will find the way

"I think this is obviously our first instruction of what we need to do when we go back in time again, we need to think hard Mason. Exactly what it is that we have to do when we find this Boy and this Girl, somehow there is a link between the past and the present, but what?"

"All I know," he replied, "is that we didn't come to this island by accident, we have been chosen to do something specific that only you and I can do. How cool is that, exactly?"

He had a fair point. They high fived each other, neither of them sure why, but they did.

The further they walked towards the X which seemed to be amongst the heavily dense trees, the more their rings were glowing to protect them.

And then, they stopped abruptly, not because they wanted to, they had to, an invisible force seemed to be stopping them from going any further. Right in front of them was a high tall rusted gate and at that point their wayfinder beeped loudly, *"You have reached your destination."*

Mason stood in front of it and had an idea. "Let's use our kneepads!" Bending down they pressed down hard to ascend quickly, lucky for them they took off without a countdown because no sooner had they become level with the gate height an invisible barrier stopped them. They banged against it and fell to the ground.

"Ouch," they both shouted, rubbing at their legs and dusting themselves down.

"I see you have found the cursed area." They turned to see Spangles walking around their feet.

"How on Earth did you get here?" exclaimed Scarlett.

"I saved my air miles."

"Ah great," said Mason, "a talking cat with a sense of humour."

"Let's take the boat back and I will tell you all about it, well mostly, or maybe just a tad," Spangles purred and led the way back out through the trees.

The brother and sister and witch's cat settled down into the boat for the journey back to the harbour at Waters End, only this time a little bit of enchantment was used and the boat rowed itself whilst Mr Spangles began his tale.

"As you know," he began, *"what we have here are a group*

of seven islands, one is habitable Waters End. The other six are not. The ancient descendants of Percy Tatterhill were keepers of these islands in the 1400s and at that time the main island was used by Pirates and King Richard the II as a storing place for hidden monies. Taxes taken from the poor and even more so when the Poll tax was introduced in 1380.

"This led to a revolt known as The Peasants Revolt in 1381. The people were fed up, they were being well and truly robbed in France and in England. The pirates were looting everywhere they could and the Seas were known not as the High Seas but as the highway robbery Seas.

Everything that was taken, well mostly all of it was hidden in the hidden bat cave and transported through many tunnels around the island. When King Richard disappeared in 1399 taken to Pontefract Castle he was then presumed dead in 1400. Not the case, he was overthrown and exiled to France to live among the peasants there, a just life for him, although nobody knew who he was.

"Or so the stories have been told.

"A great storm raged in 1397 and the pirates at that time had pilfered back all of the treasures that had been hidden here, along with all of the money belonging to the people. But the ship sank and all the crew perished. The witches at that time were blamed for the great storm and hence it became known here as Witchetty Waters.

"The witches of course did not cause the storm nor the sinking of the ship, but when they had been bought here, chained up and left for dead, they soon escaped. Together with Percy's descendants they retrieved the masses of treasure and money from the bottom of the ocean and placed it on the six islands under a heavy curse.

"It gets a lot more complicated, but suffice to say if you

could imagine another realm and say that realm was called The Realm of the clocks of time ruled by King Gregory the Great together with his wise council, a great place of wisdom that planned to correct all wrong doings, and that a cat like myself, horses and owls, all of whom are time-less and live eternally, and we go back to that realm through the portal of ticking tocking... well…"

The Beckett siblings were sitting quietly taking all of this in... "Well?" asked Scarlett.

"Some things cannot exactly be changed but the circumstances can be altered so that when the wrongs have been done then the right things can happen afterwards to correct it. So, imagine that all of the stolen monies stayed on the island and that each of the seven islands had become homes to orphans, poor people, animal sanctuaries, holy men etc. etc. Imagine also that all those happy, prosperous lives could reach out across to Europe and use the money from these stolen treasures to create peace and harmony everywhere"

"Sounds too good to be true really," said Mason.

"Only because nobody has known anything different to the world as it is now," Scarlett replied thoughtfully.

"If you could go back in time and start to make the changes with your knowledge now not known to people in the Middle Ages, then all things are possible. So basically, your tasks will be to follow the instructions just given to you, make friends, use your imagination and skills from sleight of hand trickery to foreseeing a Golden Future for all. You are the chosen two, you have protection and items that will be of great help."

"Who knows about any of this?" Scarlett asked.

"Everybody on this island, chosen ones on the mainland,

everybody really except your parents, they would worry too much!

"Oooh and Septimus Dread has no idea either. Him and his Uncle have spent many years searching for treasure that isn't on the island anymore, he isn't a mad axeman, just a bit mad."

"So... what we have to do, in a nutshell of course, is go back in time and make sure that all the poor people get back what belongs to them and make life better, and… then in the future, like now, all these islands will be put to good use, for everyone."

"Change the world, yes I like it," added Scarlett. "Well part of it anyway."

"And who knows," Mr Spangles was now preening himself, he swiped his paw behind his ears, *"Witchetty Waters could instead become Becketts Havens."*

They had now arrived back at the harbour and as they moored up Spangles jumped off. The wayfinder beeped a message, *"Congratulations, you still had 90 points left 40 over what was needed. Your test result is a pass B+."*

They were happy with that.

Beanie walked over to them, "Hello you two, little surprise for you when you get home today," he winked and carried on walking towards his cabin.

"Oooh I like surprises," said Mason.

Today had gone very well, much better than Elvira Vickery was expecting from her pupils. It was not her place to interfere with what was written, her first job was to prepare them and send them on their way. Mission accomplished.

Dino was fed up with waiting, he was getting very hungry, so yawning away he got himself up and bounded back through the forest. He had found him, that was the main thing, maybe best to report back to the others where Septimus was hiding out.

Septimus Dread was not as stupid as they all thought he was, he knew that stinking beast had been outside, he could hear his loud snoring, so he had played a waiting game all day. Wasn't exactly the quietest thing on two legs around here, so he knew it had now gone off as well.

He would hide out till nightfall and then go and get himself one of those boats and clear off away from here for a few days, wasn't anybody on the other islands. Or so he thought, but he had never been to the other islands, well he had, sort of, but… nothing there except birds, he guessed.

Strictly speaking there was nobody on the other islands. There were however Keepers of all different types and each island would be darker than the last. The Runners were the mildest of the keepers.

Unbeknown to him the easiest way to make himself known was to set foot on any of them. He took himself away from the tomb, taking a chance to make it up to the lookout tower. His cabin was a no no now, that would be the first place they would look for him.

Unaware that the cabin was no longer there anyway, his plan was the tower. Followed by a raid on the organic garden belonging to The Bakewells, then a break into their cold storage for supplies, onto the boat, and away over to the second island.

There had been plenty of wood left over and Tom had spent the last hour or so with a bit of help making a posh new 'house' for the latest members of the family. It had two rooms with a ramp going up to it enclosed with a large run all the way around, it was stuffed out with straw, bowls and foodstuff supplied by Beanie.

The new additions were three small black rabbits, the names would be left up to Scarlett and Mason.

"No way," shouted out Mason as he approached the house and found the new residents outside. He ran up to it very excited.

Scarlett smiled as she saw the new pets. "All yours bro," she laughed, she was holding out for her very own cat. A dog would have been nice, a proper dog, but Dino would have to do!

She went inside and left him to it, it had been a long day and there would be much to do tomorrow. A relaxing bath, a good book, and that would be her sorted this evening.

Dino was outside barking and talking all at once to Tom. He nodded and made his way over to find Freddie, Ted and Beanie whom he had only just left a short while ago. "Dino tracked him down," said Tom. He told them of the whereabouts of Septimus.

The four men all arranged to scout around the island at nightfall and apprehend Septimus. They would take the truck round to the back of the island with Dino sat in the back to show them the spot they had missed where the big man had been hiding out.

They also thought that it would be a good idea for Mrs Bakewell to spend the evening at No. 1 Waters End with Grace Beckett and to make Miss Vickery and Mr Greenleaf aware that there could be some 'goings on' this evening and maybe the two of them should spend their evening together just to be safe.

"Splendid," said Elvira. "We could have a bridge evening," she informed her gentlemen callers. Not intending to do anything of the sort. As soon as they left she looked into her crystal ball watching them head towards Basil's house.

She observed that once there they were a lot more truthful with him, explaining all about Septimus and that things could get a little heavy this evening.

Tut tut, she thought, if anyone on this island could sort out this big troublemaker it would be her, and she would have fun doing it.

Spinning the ball around concentrating over the forest, she soon spotted him darting through the trees and muttering to himself, "Veg, meat, boat, island, mutter, mutter, grunt," on and on he went. So that was his plan, she thought, piecing it all together, to gather himself some provisions and then take off in the night.

And take off he would, with a little bit of help from Miss Vickery and her faraway spell.

Ships that sail in the night
Propel thy speed and take thee flight
Tiny boats moored at the shore
Show this man the watery door
Up up and far away
Across the miles that's where you'll stay.
Lost at sea for weeks on end
Your mind will drive you round the bend.

She finished this off with a sprinkling of swirling dust encasing the crystal ball which was focused on the harbour.

Of course when the tomb was located that dusky evening only to be found empty apart from the coffin of the old lumberjack, the trail then led back into the forest. Dino was on high alert, sniffing and walking from side to side following the exact steps of Septimus.

From there they ended up at the lookout tower, and from there they ended up at Ted's garden which had been trampled all over and a substantial amount of fruit and veg ripped out of the ground. From there to the cold storage which had been wrenched open and the freezer lids up, showing meat and fish a plenty missing.

"Cheeky blighter," Ted raged.

And finally hot on his trail, they ended up down at the harbour mooring where the boat with the motor was no longer.

At that moment up in the sky a shout could be heard and a boat disappeared into the night clouds at great speed.

Elvira watched all in her crystal ball. Have a nice trip... Septimus. For the first time in a long time she cackled.

CHAPTER TWELVE

Once again Scarlett and Mason are transported back in time to 1377 via the portal that belongs to Elvira Vickery and once more they arrive very quickly at the destination inside the Cavern on the hill at Westings Mainland.

Totally equipped with everything to aid them plus their rings of protection and the circle of Higher Wizards and Witches in various locations watching their backs, their first mission now begins.

They must find their way towards The Coach & Horses Inn and locate the boy known as Si, he has been told to expect them. Hidden about them they have coins, nothing too large, farthings and halfpennies and silver pennies and a couple of half groats each.

Four farthings equalled one penny, two halfpennies equalled one penny, a half groat was equal to two pennies. A silver groat equal to four pennies.

Other monies would be far too high for them to be walking around with at all, a silver groat was worth four pence and then there were nobles. A ¼ noble was worth one shilling and eight *pence, a ½: 3 shillings and four pence and a noble worth six shillings and eight pence would be a small fortune.*

A skilled craftsman would probably earn six pence a day, 12 pence worth a shilling and 20 shillings worth a pound. They needed to know all of this and keep it in their minds. Keep their money well hidden, for emergency use only, and use it wisely.

They would locate Si and then Fira who would be more difficult to find. They were to be their allies, they both knew now that they had tasks to complete, none of which would be easy. Act ignorant and keep heads down, for the time being anyway.

Scarlett felt her heart beating fast, this was so surreal and the dangers here were many. Mason was talking to himself out loud with a double sided coin he was practising to a pretend audience, presenting himself as the one, the only, Mason… Master of all Magicians. She smiled at him.

If anything he could prove to be a good distraction, she thought. Her skill was a totally different one, convincing others she had the power of fore-seeing the future, and was a blessed child, a saviour. There would be a fine line between that and witchcraft, she had to tread carefully.

A small scruffy dog appeared beside them, quite thin looking and rough haired, no collar, but it seemed friendly enough and happily trotted along with them. Mason dug into his pocket where he always had a supply of biscuits and threw a couple down for the animal, it wolfed them down no problem and wagged its tail.

They all made their way down the hill towards the cobbled streets and the pub, taking care to go quietly, and doing plenty of ducking and diving along the way. They needed to suss out everything.

There were one or two stalls out on the streets, nothing very appetising to look at. Small children were sitting around looking cold and hungry just like the one they bumped into on their last visit. "Makes you realise how lucky we are," whispered Mason to his sister, she nodded in agreement.

In no time they were approaching the harbour front, and down here it was a lot more lively, it was full of pirates. They avoided eye contact, and kept themselves discreet.

"Pssst! Hither, hither." They turned to see a young lad looking about the same age as Mason beckoning to them with his hand. They walked towards him.

"Prithee, hither (Please come),"

"What is your name?" Scarlett asked him.

"Si," he replied.

She nodded. "This is Mason and I am Scarlett."

"Let's get away from the mung (crowd of people). Do you have a penny?"

"Yes," Mason said and gave one to him.

"Let's get some nesh (fresh fruit and veg) and some Earthapples (potatoes) from the voil (town) and visit the backstress (female baker). Fira always welcomes Crug (food)."

A large woman headed towards them, "Who are these Fopdoodles (simpletons)?" she asked Si.

"They're not fopdoodles," he said. "These are my cousins, come to visit." He grabbed Mason's arm and pulled him along.

"Take no notice of her she is just a blobtale (gossip)." The pair watched Si as he bought supplies. Scarlett busy observing how people worked, and talked, they had a whole new bunch of words to learn and quickly she thought. She made a mental note of all prices too.

Lastly they went to a boose (cow stall) and there they got fresh milk. All three of them walked with their arms full of ware. "People will think we are all Gunduguts (gluttons)," laughed Si.

"Where are we going?" asked Mason.

"We have a meeting with Fira, some helpers from the church, and a couple of wizards and witches, be careful of your pockets, look after your chinkers (money)," replied Si.

"The meeting is at the Cosh (small cottage) deep in the woods. Fira's lair." Once again the small dog appeared at their side.

"Don't know where this dog keeps appearing from," smiled Mason.

"Just a trundle tail (low bred dog)," said Si. "Few of them about here."

"Hoful now ha-ha."

"What's funny?" said Scarlett, too late, 'ha-ha' was a hidden ditch and both the Becketts just fell into it. Si had jumped over it.

Si looked down to them. "I told you to be hoful (careful)," he laughed. It was only a few feet down and thick soft grass so their landing wasn't too bumpy. They gathered up the fruit veg and potatoes they were carrying.

"Time for a bit of showing off Sis." They knelt down, pressed on their kneedpads and shot straight up out of the ditch again. Landing once again in a heap next to Si.

"Bit too high there brother." The dog barked running around them all.

"Do all you children of the future have such powers?" Si stared at them. "I am truly pitchkettled (puzzled)," he said.

"Only the chosen ones, namely us," Scarlett said.

145

"Yes, superpowers for heroes only," added Mason grandly.

"Hufty tuftys (braggarts)," muttered Si.

"What's that mean?" Mason whispered.

"Darned if I know," Scarlett whispered back.

"When we get back we need lessons in Medieval speak," Mason said, she agreed with him.

"Thither (that way)," Si said, pointing to the trees in the distance.

"We have to be hoful (careful) of knights on blonks (powerful horses). We need to stay hidden and especially from Knight Sir Casm, I am one of his pages and I should be working today."

They chatted away on their way through the woods, gathering all useful information on the way. Si was ten years old, he did not have parents, he was one of the 'orphaned' children that the church looked after. There were many of them, but not all members of the church helpers were very helpful.

All of the children had been abandoned by their parents who could not afford to keep and look after them, and most were set to work as soon as possible to help support the church. They each had a donge (mattress) to sleep upon, shelter in the old church, clothing and enough food to keep them alive, for this they should be very grateful.

Fira also was an orphan but was found to hold special powers and for her own protection she had been placed in the old cottage shared with witches/wizards when she reached the age of 12, and also because she was a very bellibone (pretty) lass. She was hidden away from the pirates. Fira was now almost 15 years old.

Fira and Si were very close and the nearest thing to a brother and sister as you could get, they looked out for each *other. Together they were on a mission to make life better for all the orphans, so were a very important part in the Middle ages to assist Scarlett and Mason the time travelling siblings with turning back the clock and righting this particular wrong, creating a parallel life for all.*

Most of the children were orphaned simply because the lower classes could not afford to raise their children and offered them to the Church. Children who were not orphaned quite often had short life spans.

It was very humbling listening to everything they were told. "We really do have to help you all," Scarlett said.

"Whatever it takes you can count on us, we're cool," Mason smiled.

A nyle (mist) was coming in from the sea and spreading inland. Creeping around in the mist and fog spreading a bit of gossip about the two Fopdoodles was the local blobtale gossiping to a couple of Mumpers (beggars) begging for scraps.

"Had chinkers they did, buying allsorts they were." A pair of rich strangers surely needed to watch their backs next time they showed their faces, the beggars would do anything for a bit of bellytimber (food).

The pirates' ears were pricking up too, this silly old fool of a woman could be heard all over the place. Full of squiddle (idle talk) but sometimes helpful.

"Grammary, grammary (thank you, thank you)," the beggars said, they weren't shy of a bit of thieving. The pirates were none too fussy who they stole from either, pieces of eight and plenty of rum was their motto.

"Also beware of the man of the woods, he suffers from woodness (insanity)," warned Si.

"We have one just like him," said Scarlett, visualising

Septimus Dread.

Si looked at her, "Maybe, but be careful of him, he is part beast too, a Satyr, a horse tailed man."

"Just gets better," frowned Scarlett.

They made their way further into the woods. Mason had been using his compass along the way, noting the direction from town to the start of the woods, which was simply North and from there they travelled in a North Easterly direction. The wayfinder technology did not work here, there were no satellites!

And then the way was blocked, just as it had been on the second island. Nothing that was visible, it was a barrier, unseen, that stopped them.

A dark crow could be seen on the tree in front of them and after careful study it turned and flew away. "That's eyeball the erendrake (messenger), he knows me and will tell Fira we are here," Si explained.

A short while later a rush of wind swirled up all around them. "Hurry," Si said and they rushed forward as the barrier lifted. Very quickly the wind returned and the barrier was back in place, now they could not get out and nobody else could get in.

There was a faint sound of music in the air, gentle and not from any direction. It seemed to come from all the trees, the sound like that made from a harp. The ground around the trees was smothered in circles of strange looking toadstools.

And then there was the unmistakable sound of running water. This place seemed sort of familiar, it was very much like part of the forest at Waters End, and sure enough high up in these trees there were lights which they knew belonged to fairies, and little noises in the plants showed small tree elves and goblins running about as busy as they could be.

In the middle of it all they came to the cottage known here as a cosh, and sitting outside on the branch of an oak tree was the crow they had seen before they entered through the barrier.

There was a heavy wooden door to the cottage which opened by itself allowing them all to walk inside.

They entered into a kitchen area where a large open fire had a hanging pot, Scarlett guessed by the smell that some sort of fish was cooking away. All sorts of herbs were tied in bunches and hung down from a metal rod attached to the ceiling just in front of a window that had leaded squares.

There were a few cats about the place, strange looking cats all of pure black and they stared intently at the strangers that had just walked in. Si they knew, the others they did not.

Seated at a very long table were four people, one could be taken as Fira, a young girl with pure black hair, she looked like a younger version of Elvira Vickery, striking green eyes. She had pale skin and a very pretty face. She was wearing a dark velvet dress with draping sleeves, quite plain and simple. Around her neck hung a silver skull chain embedded with two black stones.

Two women and one man were looking straight at them as if they were analysing their very souls. From their clothes they could be taken as witches and a wizard, all wore dark long flowing robes and floppy hats. Quite a theatrical sight they all looked, Scarlett thought.

The male gestured for them to sit.

"Good morrow to you all (good day). I am Tarragon, head Warlock, you have already met Druleus, head Wizard, and this is Isadora and Juniper, witches of the highest order. They're known to Fira as Dizzy Izzy and Loony Junie, and that will I'm sure become self explanatory." He smiled. "This of course is Fira." Fira smiled at them all.

"Good morrow," she said.

"Hello, I am Scarlett, this is my brother Mason. The dog is not ours, he just followed us," she said. They laid down their goods on the worktop and sat at the table with the others.

"Do you have your bubblebow Fira?" asked Tarragon. She nodded. "Please give it to the two siblings." Fira placed a small ladies' pocket book onto the table, inside it was full of information a helpful list of words from this time for the two time travellers to take away and teach themselves.

"Cool," said Mason.

"Cool? Maybe you should return the favour on your next visit. Now to business." Tarragon studied the young man.

"You are here to assist us, there is a lot to be done and it will take much time. Firstly the matter of most urgency are the orphans, but first, you need to help us with what you know."

Scarlett led the way with this one and explained everything that had happened in time gone by from now when Richard the II came to the throne in 1377, the poll tax in 1380, peasants revolt in 1381, the plundering in great amounts by pirates and the sinking of The Jolly Sea ship by a great storm in 1397, the disappearance of the King in 1399 followed by his supposed death in 1400.

Lastly, how the witches were blamed for the storm chained and taken to the main island of the set of seven and left to die, which they did not. They retrieved all of the sunken monies and treasure, and hid it all, placed invisible barriers on the smaller six islands and placed them under curse.

"We have been to the second island and there was an invisible barrier the same as you have here and there was a pair of large iron rusted gates that are locked as well."

"The King was allegedly storing all of the peasants' tax

money plus a stake of the pirates' treasure on the main island taken there by the pirates who later went back to steal it all.

The islands were overseen by some ancestors of Percy Tatterhill. He owns the islands now, the islands are known as Witchetty Waters due to the sinking of the ship and the ancient curse placed on all the islands."

All of the people in the room listened carefully to what they were being told.

"Everyone on the islands including the witches were left there, and after the storm and the sinking of the ship, the waters were avoided as dangerous." Scarlett thought that about covered it.

"Yes," agreed Mason, "everything my sister just said, can I use the toilet please?"

"Privvy (toilet) is thither (there)," pointed Fira to another door at the back of the room.

"So... we have many options... of what shall become and what shall not, what we can or cannot change… and how much of this be the truth or fadoodle (nonsense)."

Tarragon looked thoughtful… Where to begin, he pondered.

The crow tapped its beak onto the window three times indicating that a friend was awaiting at the barrier. Fira looked at the large heavy mirror standing in the corner and tapped it with her wand, it changed into an image of the woods, there she could see the members of the church coming to this meeting today.

She swirled her wand and chanted:

Enter my hidden lair
Veil lift, winds bare
Hither Thither all around
Safe on my solid ground

Meanwhile, back on Waters End the changes were taking place swiftly in the forest. The flow of water was now complete from the inlet at the hidden bay and bat cave and all the way through there was a main stream, waterfall and many other water outlets. There were fresh fish swimming in the streams.

One part was completely taken over by the Sprites now and music could be heard all around just as it could around the woods surrounding Fira.

This section of the island was to be a place of magical hope for all who entered into it, where dreams would come true, and wishes could be granted.

Behind this area where the clearing and the lookout tower was, there was to be a sanctuary for all unusual species of animals not found anywhere else on the planet, and this part had its first occupant as Dino the Dragondoggen was busy with his very large tail clearing away brambles and undergrowth. The tower was now his home.

If all went to plan, then island number two would lose all of its runners to make way for the biggest orphanage ever seen. The runners would become part of the *Camp of Curious Creatures,* as would the sand duners. Their new sanctuary would be with Dino.

Islands number three, four, five, six and seven also housed very unusual animals guarding them, all of these should one day find their home at Waters End too.

And so it was decided at Fira's lair that day, the things that could be changed would start with Scarlett and Mason bringing back in time certain items from the future that could be put to good use in 1377.

Also, as neither witches or wizards nor Fira could travel into Westings safely, then it would be up to the other concealed lesser witches and wizards to aid the Beckett siblings with their first quest. They needed to find a way to get over to the islands in 1377.

Once there, find a secure place that would not be known to anyone and prepare it to remove some of the stolen treasures and hidden monies that shortly in the future the pirates would be hiding. The island was already concealing tunnels that had been dug out and were already being used for contraband.

Once back in the present time they needed to find out the name of Percy's first descendant. He would need to be approached before being appointed island keeper.

A hearty meal was dished up after an afternoon of talking and decision making of Spitchcock (eel in breadcrumbs), hot potatoes and vegetables, as well as a large jug of Adam's ale (water) and some hum for the adults (strong beer/spirit mix).

"Show us some of your skills young Mason, let us see what you can do," Tarragon said, it did not sound like a request more like an order.

Mason was in his element using cards and dice, his double sided coin, making things appear and disappear and showing off some very good skills with a rope trick that had them all puzzled. Everyone clapped when he had finished. "Very good, use your tricks wisely to cause a distraction."

For a young person with just the power of illusion he was very talented.

"How will we get on board a ship?" Scarlett asked.

"The power of your knees should get you both up into the crow's nest, you will need the disguise of a boy Scarlett."

Isadora and Juniper both piped up in unison, "If we may."

In the past, yes in the past
On ship you sail, ship you sail
To Waters End, yes Waters End
You both be male, both be male
You hide the loot, yes hide the loot
To the future go, the future go
Find it there, yes find it there
Because you know, because you know
In the past, yes in the past
The treasures bring, treasures bring
Build the home, yes build the home
The children sing, children sing.
On island two, yes island two
Will orphans stay, orphans stay
You must not fail, must not fail
To save the day, yes save the day.

The two witches then twirled their wands in the air and caught all the words they had just spoken poetically, and with a flick of the wrist the poem of guidance was placed into the notebook given to them earlier by Fira.

"It is time for you all to leave," Fira said suddenly. She stood up and the door opened for all of the guests, nobody spoke another word. The occupants of the cottage looked at them intently once more.

"Well, it's all a lot clearer now, goodbye then." Mason couldn't wait to leave, boredom had set in a long time ago. Scarlett just nodded and walked out of the door, as did Si, the Church helpers, and the small dog.

Once again they were seen out of the barrier which promptly went straight back up again. "You know your way." Si bade them goodbye and very quickly walked off. Suddenly it felt very alien in here, Mason picked up the dog.

"Leg it?" Scarlett didn't need asking again. They ran at super speed through the woods and did not look back, feeling that all eyes were on them, and they would be right.

Then, they were stopped in their tracks. Suddenly standing right in front of them was the large old gossip of a woman from the town, with her were two scruffy looking men, at a guess they looked like tramps. Scarlett and Mason were startled by them.

"What do you want?" Scarlett asked.

The old woman cackled. "You need a good yerd (beat with a rod). Pair of fopdoodles," she spat at them.

"These are them, loaded with chinkers (money) they are," she turned to the pair of Mumpers (beggars). "Go on you pair of Poop-Noddy's (fools), search them, go on," she yelled.

"Tell you what," Mason said, taking a couple of coins out of his pocket, "if you can see them, you can take them."

He held out his hand with the coins, one of the old beggars grabbed at them. Very quickly with sleight of hand they disappeared.

"What kind of reaks (practical joke) was that? Come here," the man angrily tried to grab Mason. Far too slow, Mason side stepped bent on his knees and jumped fifteen feet into the air right over their heads.

Scarlett copied and did the same, leaving the three of them dumb struck. "Not a good idea to mess with the Magician or the Fore-seeing one, we will take the light from the sky for your actions."

She slyly placed her gloves onto her hands and rubbed them together creating a blinding light. "Be gone with you all," she shouted. Mason copied her actions and once again another

155

blinding light shone into their faces.

"You heard her, we won't say it again." The three of them turned and fled back the way they had come. What were these creatures?

"Take the light from the sky?" Mason laughed at her.

"Oh didn't I say?" Scarlett smiled at him. "A total eclipse is happening tomorrow, and it will fit in with our plans just nicely."

"Oh, well wicked, can't wait."

They could not resist running rings round the escaping would be thieves before shooting off towards the top of the hill.

In the distance they could still hear the large woman screaming, served her right.

And meanwhile somewhere adrift in the English Channel was a small boat bobbing up and down. In it was a wet, tired and very troubled man grunting and moaning and groaning. Septimus Dread was busy throwing raw fish and raw meat over the side of the small boat, no good to him now. Apart from water all he had was fruit and vegetables.

He had known better weeks. "Damn them, damn them all," he cursed to himself. He would be back and they would all know about it. A seagull just made his day that little bit worse when a plop from a great height landed on his head.

When they arrived back at Waters End village Scarlett phoned Percy Tatterhill. She needed a little bit of information. She was glad she made the call because she now had some interesting facts that they had not known before, it would be useful to them.

CHAPTER THIRTEEN

The next morning, they found themselves once again crash landed onto the cavern floor at Westings Mainland, 1377.

Now they were used to the route down to the harbour and back again to the awaiting horses, this much was familiar to them. Today though, no Si or Fira, they were on their own.

Scarlett had been using her time back at home wisely and had mentally noted all timeline events for the period 1377 onwards which she would use to their advantage. For instance, she knew that there was going to be a total eclipse of the sun in just under an hour from now.

After her conversation with Percy Tatterhill the night before she now knew that the name of the descendant they were looking for was Edmund Tatterhill and that he had actually taken the job of keeping the islands several months before Richard the II became King. It was in fact the pirates themselves that placed him there first, looking after their hoards of treasures and monies.

The islands were afterwards claimed from the pirates as part of The British Isles and all valuables there were 'taxed' as such, a little bit of a twist from the original rumours. Edmund was to remain there eventually under direct employ overseeing all in the name of the King.

So, all they had to do was get on board a ship and locate Edmund and his family. At least now there was the starting of a plan.

The eclipse would provide the perfect cover, it was the major distraction that could afford them the time for a minute or two to board the Jolly Sea Ship that was due to sail out.

All they had to do was get down to the harbour, and wait. It would be their first time on the island as it used to be in the Middle Ages, so it wouldn't be that familiar to them.

Using their fast feet, they shot from the cavern to the edge of the town in no time at all, skidding to a halt before they reached the cobbled streets.

Just as before they had located their clothes in the chest in the barn back at Waters End, the garb came under 'Motley crew' pirate wear, which basically meant it was a right mixture of colours and materials. The wigs, beards and moustache, they now wore was perfect for concealing their earphones, and the eye patches did not look out of place. They had everything they needed.

They easily mingled with everyone else around the harbour and noticed that an awful lot of barrels and wooden crates were being loaded up onto the ship.

"Shiver me timbers," Mason said, just for the hell of it.

Scarlett gave a sneaky look at her watch. "Thirty minutes to go," she whispered to her brother.

Once again they noticed that the gossip woman was among the people milling around. She was looking very concerned, and looking up at the sky. Scarlett was sure that by now everybody for miles around would know of the two strangers with powers, and not to cross them.

"Hither, hither," a pirate beckoned them over. "Move these along," he rolled a barrel towards Scarlett, she then rolled it to her brother and he carried on to the man in front of him.

Everyone was too busy to take much notice of them, the sky was getting very dark. "Probably a storm brewing up," someone shouted.

"Aye," shouted another. The two kids had no problem shifting these large barrels along. All the food they had been eating since they moved onto the island really was making them super fit.

Last night's delight had been a super stew with enrichment dumplings. Huge great things they were and inside them were marbled stripes of colour.

So, the plan was now, as soon as it became pitch black to leg it up this ramp and into the ship, up onto the main deck and a countdown of three on their insoles. A giant leap should get them up into the crow's nest, there they would stay until they reached the island.

Just over ten minutes to go.

A dark shadow passed over them and the harbour was getting so dark now it was turning into night. "What's going on here?" a panic started to fill the place, nobody here would know what an eclipse was.

"It's witchcraft."

"Don't talk fadoodle (nonsense)."

"Oi'll be pitchkettled (puzzled)."

"Almost there," Scarlett said to Mason. "One more minute."

"Juvament, juvament (help, help)," a woman cried in fear. By now everyone was trying to take cover and hiding wherever they could. "It's the end of the world."

And then, total blackness. "Quick, run." Scarlett grabbed Mason by the hand and they shot up the wooden ramp and into the Ship, it was pitch black in here and they were banging into everything.

"Quick, use your gloves," Mason said. They both grabbed them out of their deep pockets rubbed them together and everywhere lit up.

They ran down the centre of the ship, either side had oars and wooden benches, until they came to wooden stairs. Up they ran, another set of wooden stairs got them to the deck of the ship. They kept their gloves on and lit up the area until they reached the bow of the ship and the main mast. Getting on their knees and in position, they pressed down hard, "1... 2... 3... jump." They grabbed onto the frame of the crow's nest and scrambled inside.

Rubbing their hands together, the light went out and they sat and waited for daylight to return.

The large woman had seen these bright lights before that she just saw shoot upwards, she cowered back down behind the barrels left strewn on the harbour.

"How cool was that," Mason was catching his breath.

"Awesome," his sister replied. It was both dangerous and exciting.

Within a few minutes, the daylight once more came back. Sailors and pirates started to scrabble out of their hiding places and headed straight into the Coach and Horses Inn after hammering on the door. A fair few rums were going to be tipped down their necks before they did anything else that day.

"They made the sky dark, they made the sky dark, I told you, I told you," cried the woman. Convinced they had both shot up towards the heavens. She looked completely off her head with madness.

The ship was very late leaving that day, and by the time the pirates took their leave from the Coach and Horses Inn, they were holding each other up. The Captain was in slightly better shape and got them all on board.

Mason stood up in the crow's nest and had a marvellous crossing, it was pretty awesome with the 360 degree vision. Eventually he called out, "Land ahoy."

The ship turned into the Hidden Bay.

The island looked very different, there was an awful lot of greenery everywhere. Once they were off the ship they would take off and hide, no problems losing themselves with all these trees. Each person that got off rolled a barrel in front of them, pushing it towards the bat cave. This much did look familiar.

They followed each other down and into the edge of the cave pushing their barrels.

"Where you be off to?" someone shouted as they walked to the back of the cave.

"Privvy," called back Mason.

"Oh aye," came the drunken reply.

They searched around hoping that the trapdoor would be in the cave, and it was. They opened the lid and dropped themselves inside, using their gloves for light they walked as fast as their legs would go searching for the other end of the tunnel. After a few minutes they found the other end, lifted the lid and made their way out.

In years to come Septimus Dread would live here, his Lumberjack Uncle built their cabin right here over this tunnel on purpose.

They were amongst many trees in the forest. Using his compass Mason led them to what would normally be their home.

Of course, there was only land there, no houses anywhere on the beach either, just sand trees and storage buildings. The distant hill where the horses would normally drop them back to the present was there, but without the horses, they would only appear at the mainland, this was the drop off point.

"You do realise we have to find a hiding place for us, wait until the ship leaves, go back to the bat cave, search for gold and any monies, get that back here and put it somewhere that exists today and in the future to retrieve it?"

"Course, no worries," Mason grinned.

"So, even if we do all of that," Scarlett replied, "tell me, how do we get back?"

"To Westings?"

"Yes, to Westings."

At this moment in time, neither of them knew.

They took themselves towards the distant hill knowing that all that was there was open fields, no pirates, they would hide in the open so to speak.

On reaching the bottom they used the power of their insoles to run with the wind to the top. It was a great vantage point, they sat and they thought, and thought some more.

From here everything was visible and with the aid of the 360 degree vision of the eye patches, it was quite a stunning view. All of the islands could be seen, it was quite a clear day now, and also the ship was just visible so they would know when it set sail and left.

They needed to find Edmund and his family, and form a solid plan. "I think I have it," Scarlett suddenly said excitedly.

She explained her idea to Mason and he nodded in agreement.

They pondered for a few moments to think about it and make sure there were not any flaws. Neither of them could think of any, it could work.

When they first arrived at Waters End, the stream and waterfall did not run with water, all the ways had been blocked and it had been cleared and brought back to life by the sprites. If they could locate the waterfall now, she was sure that behind the foliage there would be a small cavern, the perfect place to hide the treasures. It would not be difficult getting behind the water flow in 2016 to get the booty back out.

They patiently sat at the top of the hill for three hours until finally the ship sailed away. It was dark when they got back down into the forest. They walked quietly, keeping their ears peeled with the help of the earphones trying to locate Edmund Tatterhill.

It took them almost forty minutes. They heard him from a long distance and could see everything all around them, the eye patches were an excellent invention by Marvello, nobody would catch them unawares.

Back on the other side of the island almost and tucked into the trees there was a small hut and outside there was a roaring fire. Two long rods were either side from which a pot was hanging and food was cooking, they were both hungry. A few people were walking around.

Walking towards the house, Mason called out, "Edmund Tatterhill?"

The man turned around and looked at them both. "You

missed the ship," he said, eyeing them suspiciously.

"We are not pirates," explained Scarlett. They walked over to introduce themselves and settled down into what would be one very long story.

They all sat with bowls of a hot stew and bread around the camp fire. All of them slept outside in a circle with the warmth of the fire and huddled under blankets. The children had sat wide eyed listening to everything they were being told, the adults sat wide eyed too, it was some tale.

Early the next morning the Tatterhill family and Beckett children set out to seek the waterfall and to see if it was possible to put their plan into action.

From now on Edmund Tatterhill would be happy to guard the treasures and monies, knowing that in the future him and his family would be safe from the storm that was to happen and they would play an important part in history for the good of all.

And find the waterfall they did, it was dry of water and the entrance practically hidden behind ivy and creepers as expected. Behind the foliage was a large rock cavern, this would house endless treasure which would never be found because almost as quickly as Edmund would fill it, it would disappear. Taken from the future time by Scarlett and Mason who in turn would take it back to the mainland and give it to Tarragon.

They would be careful to take only about a third of all treasures hidden in the bat cave. It would not matter because one day in the future all of it would be recovered anyway, the storm would still happen, and the ship would still sink. Not everything could be rewritten, nor should it.

There would be no second chances for some people.

Hidden amongst their clothing, Scarlett and Mason had

their bags which would hold countless coins. They could use these today to transport everything they could and place it inside the waterfall ready to collect as soon as they got home. After that the job would be taken over by Edmund and his family, the keepers of the secrets.

But how would they get home? The thought kept nagging at Scarlett.

Once inside the bat cave, Edmund jemmied off the secured lids of the square wooden boxes and opened them up. They were cram packed with gold, silver, coins, jewels, a proper hoard of treasure taken from here and Europe by pirates everywhere and Knights.

"No wonder so many people are poor," said Scarlett.

"These will be moved when the pirates return, put down into other tunnels where they will be locked away, making room for more. This is just a holding bay," explained Edmund.

So, they figured a plan, to remove as many coins as was possible and tip them into their bags. The more they could take today the better, and the bags being bottomless pits and weightless made today THE day to shift most of it.

Edmund set to bringing as many rocks as he could from the beach which would be hidden almost at the bottom of the boxes to replace the weight.

They worked hard and long and when they finished, once more the boxes were secured again as before.

They took the hoard to the covered waterfall where they scrambled through the foliage and went right to the back of the cavern. Tipping everything out, they covered it over with dirt, there was no more they could do.

Every few days, Edmund's wife and four children were allowed back onto the mainland to get supplies of their choosing. Edmund was to remain here permanently on guard.

So it was decided that Scarlett and Mason would take the place of two of his children on the next trip out. They were provided with clothes, the pirates never paid heed to them, they should not be noticed.

"Can I ask, did you blacken the sky yesterday?" Edmund was still very pitchkettled (puzzled) by that.

Scarlett laughed, "No we didn't," and went on to explain what an eclipse was, but assured Edmund there would be no more for a very long time.

So it was that the pirates returned, went about their business moving crates and barrels and Mrs Agnes Tatterhill and her four 'children' slipped on board without any bother for the journey to the mainland. They went down into the corner of the lower deck keeping themselves to themselves.

Reaching Westings mainland, they disembarked and went their separate ways, all giving a silent nod.

Today, they walked at a normal pace not wanting to draw any attention to themselves. It was much quieter than it usually was, the effect of the darkened sky had frightened everyone and some were still afraid to come out of their homes.

They headed towards the hill. Once more they were reunited with the little dog, it looked very happy to see them both, wagging its tail and jumping all around. Mason once again rewarded it with biscuits from his bag.

"I wonder?" Scarlett said.

"Wonder what?" Mason looked at her.

"Do you think it would be possible to take him back with us?"

"Well, he is a stray without a real home here isn't he?"

Mason said. There was only one way to find out, picking him up they both raced like the wind up to the waiting horses.

"Hold him tightly," Scarlett shouted out as they climbed onto the timeless horses, whoosh, they were gone.

And in seconds they were back, and so too was the dog. Once on the grass they checked him over, he was running around, oblivious he had just gone over 600 years into the future. "Wicked," Mason said. They walked down the hill today, choosing not to run with the wind.

Scarlett said, "Let's take him to Basil tonight to check him over, and then I'm thinking a few white lies, a bit of help from Beanie as to where he came from, and then we get to keep him?"

Elvira as usual had overseen their safe return, plus the 'extra'. This little dog had no protection and she would be interested to see how this panned out. It could open up a whole new angle, if, and it was a big if, the dog came to no harm.

They dropped the dog, Basil was happy to give it a once over and keep hold of it for the night. He was a doctor not a vet, but he too was thinking along the same lines as Elvira.

Immediate problem, how would they explain being away for all this time? They would have to wing that one. Walking into No. 1 Waters End, their Mother simply turned to them and said, "Hello, did you have a good day?" They were stumped.

This meant they could be gone for a whole week and nobody would be any the wiser, or a year even. Scary, thought Scarlett. Way cool, Mason thought.

"By the way, your rabbits need cleaning out Mason," his Mother shouted as he was running upstairs.

"Fadoodle (nonsense)," he shouted. He needed to invent something for that, he thought.

She had not batted an eyelid at the clothes they had turned up in today. They were getting themselves into a couple of tracksuits and couldn't wait to get to the waterfall, they needed to desperately know that the plan had worked. After a few moments they shot out of the house again and raced off to the forest.

They were almost tripping over each other in their haste to get there, and soon enough the sound of running water could be heard. The strange musical noise of this enchanted place was everywhere.

"Please be there, please, please be there," Mason was begging out loud.

"It has to be," Scarlett assured him. And there in front of them was the waterfall, crystal clear water running down everywhere. They climbed up to it, crossing their fingers.

They quickly side stepped into the water and behind it peering into the rock cavern walking towards the back, the location they had tipped the bags out. Mason put his gloves on and rubbed his hands together, whilst Scarlett gently moved away all the Earth that had settled in this spot. From side to side she swept it, and there it was, a whole pile of coins, two huge bagful's. They quickly scooped all of it up.

"High five," he said. This moment was just huge, they could now start changing history.

The immensity of what was now possible was not

lost on Scarlett, this was big, so much now depended on this. The pair of them scooped up all the coins, dropping them once again into their bags ready to deliver to Druleus and Tarragon, back in time.

CHAPTER FOURTEEN

It was Christmas Eve at Waters End and after the last few weeks of bedlam, it was time to have a week or two off and all the family were looking forward to a nice break together.

There were several presents under the tree, some very odd shaped boxes and parcels and it was all very festive looking especially with the big log fire. The oddest looking sausage rolls were being baked and mince pies with green edges were cooling on a rack.

There was going to be a bit of a get together, several of the mainlanders were coming over for the evening and Ted and Nancy were throwing a 'knees up' party at The Village Stores.

A few other special guests were coming along too, so all in all this was the place to be tonight.

Grace was busy making jellies and a large bowl of punch, Scarlett was sure it wasn't actually supposed to be bubbling. Nancy would be busy with her cookery and so was Elvira, the men would collect it all and take it to the stores.

Her Mother was looking more and more a mixture of Nancy and Elvira every day, Scarlett observed, and her Father too had changed a lot. He was becoming more and more like the other men on the island, sort of… well sort of… she wasn't sure what, it was like one huge family at this place, like they had all been there for hundreds of years.

The men were also busy decorating several outside trees with lights. The woods were to be out of bounds this evening, because some knew of the creatures that lived deep inside, but some did not, and best it stayed that way, especially for the likes of Patrick Hinger.

Mason was in his element because his long time best friend Charlie had been staying here for the past few days. He was going back later on this evening on the return ferry. The pair of them had been as thick as thieves, up to all sorts, there had been plenty of flashes and banging coming from the shed outside.

They had camped out in the barn, been fishing with Ted in the new large trawler boat that was now moored at the bay, and helped to build a tree house with Freddie Spinner and Tom Beckett. It was awesome.

Scarlett and Mason had both agreed though, that the waterfall, the enchanted part of the forest and Dino were all to be out of bounds. There were definitely secrets that only the siblings would share, as for the time travelling, that was a definite no-no.

Charlie had brought with him his latest 'toy', a machine that picked up signals from outer space and beyond, it would beep like crazy sometimes. "You have aliens here," Scarlett heard him tell Mason many times. Yeah right, she thought.

Deep in the Channel waters, Charlie's little machine was actually causing a disturbance between the rhythmic beep from a deep underground cavern and the *The Time Warp Ship* who had dropped the cargo there.

The ship's dashboard was beeping all out of zinc with the container in the cavern. This was not good, not good at all, it was causing the Captain of the craft much concern.

Tonight, Dazlin who was also coming to the island party was bringing with him the high tech satellite dish/signal receiver for Mason as promised some time ago. Mason had also pestered his Dad for a machine like the one Charlie had too, and a very powerful telescope.

Scarlett decided that this would be a great time to just disappear with the little family pet dog, who now favoured her company above the others. They strolled along the beach together.

He seemed to be just doing fine, Basil had checked him all over and apart from needing a lot of TLC and plenty of nourishment, he was okay. Beanie saw to all of the injections, worming and all other delights that a pooch needed. He was approximately a year old, and not in bad shape.

And *he* now had a name too, *Astro*. Scarlett thought that was perfect for him, she had claimed him as her dog and he was pretty cool with that.

She pulled her hat down over her ears, it had been a present from Nancy and when she wore it, she just seemed to relax and kick back, it made her take a little time out for herself. It even lit up around the edges. Girl and dog ambled along quite peacefully.

"It's your turn," Mason said to Charlie and handed him Big-Ears, the largest of his three pet rabbits and the large black hat. Mason was being deliberately smug, because he had perfected this trick over the last few weeks, and to be fair Charlie didn't have a clue how to do it. He was paying him back. Charlie loved showing off with his supersonic signal gadget thing and Mason had yet to get the hang of that.

Good friends having a bit of harmless fun over the holiday, for a little while Mason was back in childish mode, and enjoying it. No powers, just a kid.

Cecily Springbocker, the Head Librarian was bringing with her tonight a book that Scarlett had requested. It had been a follow up book to those she had previously borrowed from the Library, this one was entitled *The Church and the Orphanage – Witchetty Waters*.

Sophia Bonetti from *Contessa Alessa* was bringing gifts with her this evening, as was Marvello from *Illusion confusion*. Percy Tatterhill had something very important that he would be bringing along as well.

King Gregory the Great and the wise council had sat at their very long table in *The Realm of the Clocks of Time* and had been busy re-writing one particular piece of history. One wrong had been righted and as such had altered the course and outcome of one certain event.

When they had finished they had placed a seal on the document and had summoned Mr Spangles to the portal of ticking tocking based on the second island to come and retrieve the document which he had. It was now in the possession of Elvira Vickery who would also be bringing a gift to the party this evening.

Under the sand, the sand duners had all scarpered away, taking themselves off around the other side of the island out of the way for a day or so, where Dino had remained also. The sprites had stayed inside their trees, hibernating.

The Runners on island two were very excited, they had much to report.

Back in time there had been much to'ing and fro'ing and it had been decided very swiftly that following the Great dark sky event, very much helped along by a gossiping woman and some beggars, that it had been a sign from the Gods that they were not happy.

So, two special children with powers had been sent as a warning that things had to change. The hidden lesser witches and wizards in mainland Westings, who appeared as ordinary folk, backed the claims that they too had seen the powers performed, adding fuel to the fire.

The Church helpers claimed the powered children, The Magician and The Fore-seeing one, had visited and insisted that a proper orphanage should be built on one of the great islands and swiftly with real amenities and staff.

It was also claimed that all local people shall be employed to build this magnificent building and they should not be taxed heavily anymore, they should be stopped a token amount to put into the local community.

There were many wrong doers that did not want this to happen, but they had to remain silent for it was a threat to all that next time the sky would remain dark forever by the wrath of the Gods.

The building began, the Church had acquired much money through 'fund raising', it was rumoured to cover the cost of this venture.

This pleased the Royalty and the Knights and they even agreed on a donation.

A meeting was held at Fira's Lair.

Things of the future would need to change. They were aware that the witches and wizards that were chained and held at Waters End in 1397 would be the lessers in the mainland. It also made perfect sense that these were the ones responsible for securing the treasures and placing them under curse on six uninhabited islands.

There would be no need now to place anything on island two as it would also be inhabited, by the orphans, and also by Isadora and Juniper, also the Church helpers, and Fira and Si.

Their meeting concluded that a message be sent to King Gregory, giving permission to start re-writing this part of history.

And so it was done, the sealed envelope given to Scarlett and Mason Beckett to take back and pass onto Elvira Vickery.

Edmund Tatterhill could not help but smile as every bagful of coins he left at the waterfall was then taken and given to the Highest order of Witches and Wizards and relocated to the workers he could see on the next island.

What goes around comes around, it was called karma.

He did not know it yet but for all the good he and his family were doing, one day they would be greatly rewarded. No longer 'prisoners' here, but would be heirs to all of the islands, they would belong to them, for many hundreds of years to come.

The ferry was making its way over from mainland Westings to Waters End, and for one evening only, there were two extra passengers who had made a long journey with the aid of special permissions from King Gregory.

On board the boat tonight was also Druleus and Tarragon, who although both blessed with eternal life and immortality, were still based back in the Middle Ages as there was still plenty to do as Scarlett and Mason were to find out. They had been granted time passage today.

So, tonight was a special meeting, and a reunion also with some special friends they had not seen for hundreds of years. Namely Fira, Isadora and Juniper, who had left the sanctuary of Fira's Lair back in 1379 for a new home at the magnificent orphanage, when it had been completed.

Also, young Si had been given a special status in the witching world and for all his dedicated work at the orphanage was given a Merit of Eternity life time as well. This meant he would forever be at the Orphanage which had enough funds to support itself through all of time. He had grown into a young man in his mid twenties and pretty much stayed at that age. Mentally he was very wise now.

There were many surprises in store tonight, for everyone. Most of them were good.

The ferry let out two large hoots and slowly turned in toward the harbour at Waters End. Let the party begin!

Scarlett had to make her way back home in a hurry after seeing the Ferry lit up and on its way across. She had been totally chilled out with her little dog.

Now, after a quick shower she was getting ready into her party dress, and slapping on a little bit of make-up and fixing her hair. Vanity had never been her strong point, nature had given her a head start, she was fair of face and did not need all the enhancement.

Twenty minutes later she was done, Astro barked at her. "You approve," she laughed. Awkwardly, she struggled, even with small heels she felt clumsy.

"Are you two ready?" she called out and knocked at her brother's door. She peeked in and caught them preening their hair with gel, collars up, outdoing each other to look cool. She quietly closed the door again and went downstairs, smiling to herself.

Her Mum was standing in the hall applying her lipstick, had she dyed her hair? "You look nice Mum." Her Mother turned to face her. "Wow, bright red lips, very… nice." Scarlett herself had opted for a pale pink, something a lot more subtle.

The phone rang. "I'll get it," Scarlett said. It was a voice she did not recognise on the other end.

"Bring your brother to the Hidden Bay in 30 minutes… please," the phone hung up.

Hmmm, she thought, who was that? Running upstairs, she got her 'special bag' and placed her insoles inside it, also Mason's pair. She had confiscated them while Charlie was here just in case Mason had the urge to show off. There was too much at stake.

She went to her brother's room and called him out. "What shall I tell Charlie?"

"Tell him you have a surprise for him and will see him soon." They were both whispering.

Their Dad was waiting at the bottom of the stairs for them. "Off we all go then, you ready Charlie?" he shouted up the stairs.

"Just coming," he shouted down, leaving a parting gift in his friend's bed of a 'prickler', a little something he had picked up off the internet. As soon as you touched it, a sensation like stinging nettles but fifty times worse would escape from it. He laughed out loud before leaving the room.

"This is one amazing island," Charlie said as he bounded down the stairs. "You're well lucky Mason."

"Thanks," his friend said.

"Ferry is here, let's go meet them all," Scarlett said, in a hurry.

Loud music could be heard coming from Ted and Nancy's Village Store. Waters End had sprung to life tonight, everywhere was lit up with coloured lights, and the trees had lights and decorations hanging from them. A look inside showed that there was an abundance of food and drink.

"What is that noise playing?" Charlie laughed.

"Nothing wrong with a bit of 60s music," Grace smiled, bopping away as she walked!

And off the ferry they came, ladies first, Sophia Bonetti, Cecily Springbocker, followed by Dazlin, with the large dish, Patrick Hinger followed, and then Percy Tatterhill, Marvello, Druleus and Tarragon.

"Is this a fancy dress party?" whispered Charlie to Mason.

Elvira made her way towards them accompanied by Basil, Beanie and Freddie. It was a full house, but there would also be some extra guests, many of them in fact.

Mason and Scarlett gave each other a quizzed look, how did the wizard and warlock from the past get here?

Percy came over to Scarlett bidding her good evening and handed her an envelope. "Put it in your bag," he said. Elvira approached too and gave her another one, followed by Sophia Bonetti handing her a small package, all of them did this discreetly.

"Don't you have somewhere to be?" Percy winked. "We will keep your friend entertained until you return."

"Charlie is it?" Percy said loudly. "Think Dazlin here could do with a hand." Charlie didn't need asking twice. What was this he wondered, not your usual satellite dish and what was that attached to it?

Distractions were taking place everywhere. "Off you go," nodded Percy.

Scarlett and Mason quietly snuck off behind the Stores. "Here," Scarlett said, handing Mason both his gloves and his insoles, a minute later they sped off.

With no time to spare, they arrived and stopped just before The Hidden Bay. A beep was heard inside one of the envelopes, the smaller one that Percy had given them. Scarlett opened it and inside was a small screen a bit like the wayfinder, an X was flashing on it, they walked towards it.

There they found a small boat, they got into it and

the screen indicated with arrows towards the second island.

Rowing quickly with one oar each they made their way over. "Take over a minute," Scarlett said and opened the larger envelope given to her by Elvira.

It had inside a sealed document which read:-

To Scarlett and Mason Beckett

I, King Gregory the Great and the Wise Council from the Realm of the clocks of time
Hereby announce
History has been re-written on this day
January 20th 1379
An orphanage has been completed
So in the great storm of 1397
This island will never be cursed
Please unlock the gates
The barrier is no more
The first wrong has been righted.

~

Scarlett had just read the contents out loud to her brother. "That is just so... wicked," he said. She couldn't agree more. This was the best Christmas present... ever.

Waiting for them at the other end was a funny little reception committee. Standing on the beach was Mr Spangles and in front of him standing to attention were small rows of odd looking creatures.

The Runners were now preparing to leave the island, as their job here was now done, they were no longer needed. They were going to be going over to Waters End where their new home would be where Dino was, at the *Camp of Curious Creatures*.

The Chief Runner handed Mr Spangles his collar, having already given him his final report.

Spangles gave it back to him. *"You earned it,"* he purred.

"Come," Spangles said to the siblings, they followed him to the trees and back to where the gate stood. This time there was no barrier around it. *"Look in your package,"* Spangles told Scarlett. She opened the gift that Sophia Bonetti had given her and inside were two intricately carved pieces of gold metal in the shape of skulls, she gave one to Mason.

They each held one up to either gate and it creaked open, and then, the gate dissolved. The trees all around parted and made way to a long beautiful path. She put the keys back in her bag.

It was lit up all the way along with old fashioned street lamps leading to the most magnificent building you could only imagine.

Spangles beckoned to them to follow him along the path.

CHAPTER FIFTEEN

So, history had been re-written, there was no treasure hidden on island two and it had never been cursed in the new series of events.

The gates still had to be unlocked and this could only be done by Scarlett and Mason Beckett, the keeper of the keys for island number two. It could only ever have been unlocked by them as the chosen ones.

All six islands had gates from 1367 onwards, the invisible curses came later. Now, these gates had just been opened.

So from the inside looking out, the island had only ever been accessed by going around the back by ship, with just a view of the Channel, with a small beach and high cliffs either side. The gate at the end of the path would not open, but now it was fully open.

From the front it had appeared unoccupied, not so anymore. Waters End was now visible, and a vast beach and harbour was available.

And on its way was the ferry from Waters End, there were many more guests to collect now. Spangles floated up and rapped on the large door knocker three times. This magnificent building was the new orphanage, in an alternative world it had been here since 1379, but now showing for the first time in this lifetime.

The large doors opened by themselves and Scarlett and Mason were met by Isadora and Juniper, who looked exactly the same as they did back in 1377.

Behind them stood Fira who was now a very beautiful young lady who looked to be in her mid twenties, but no more. Finally stood a young man beside her, also in his twenties.

"You got my phone call then?" he grinned.

"Si?" said Scarlett.

"Yes," he smiled. Mason looked at him, no longer somebody of his own age and he thought twice about telling him he now knew what Hufty Tuftys were!

"I think we have a party to go to," said Fira and with that lots and lots of excited children ran towards the door.

It was quite a moment watching them, very happy, well clothed and just the same as any other kids they both knew. There was nothing dreary about this place, nothing at all.

Everybody made their way down the long well-lit path, even in the dark you could see that the gardens were beautiful.

Where the gate had stood minutes earlier was an archway perfectly formed by tree branches and on the other side of that was another path the same that had not been there before leading down to a small harbour now similar to that of Waters End.

The small boat was no longer there, Scarlett had a feeling that the runners and Mr Spangles had hijacked it.

The ferry was all lit up and Fira invited Si, Scarlett and Mason to sit with her. She was different now, still very witch like, but neither spoke riddled words from the Middle Ages.

"So, how do you feel after completing your first quest?" Fira asked.

"Very grateful to have been a part of it," said Scarlett.

Mason nodded, "What she just said," he smiled. "Awesome, great."

Fira looked at them and thought a moment before she would ask the next question. Thinking better of it she decided to wait and let them enjoy the party.

The two witches were keeping the kids entertained on the short journey from one island to the other. Once again they were speaking in unison, one repeating after the other one, but it was as if they already knew what the other one was going to say, they were uncanny.

Waters End, yes Waters End
An enchanting place, enchanting place
With pixies and sprites, pixies and sprites
The runners race, runners race
A dragon dog, yes dragon dog
Sand duners lie, sand duners lie
There's sprites in trees, sprites in trees
The cat can fly, cat can fly.
Septimus Dread, yes Septimus Dread
Is far from dead, far from dead.

And so, with a little mix of music bought in from the orphanage, the evening was one full of laughter and much talking, game playing, and a little bit of drinking from the adults. Percy had bought a few bottles from his own personal collection.

In one area congregated the wizards and witches and Percy.

Patrick could be heard above everybody else, "Course if you ask me they should never have put the ship route behind that next island, you say it's open now? Well why did they not do it years ago is what I want to know, didn't even know there was an orphanage there, did you?" he was asking no-one in particular because nobody would look at him.

Scarlett, Mason, Dazlin and Charlie sat at a table outside catching up all the news from the mainland. Charlie and Mason were making the most of the next couple of hours together. "Do you think I can come back at Easter?"

Mason laughed, "You bet."

There were over 130 children here tonight,

running around everywhere, so happy, and now they had another island they would be allowed to visit, even bigger than their own.

The small boat at the hidden bay had been left tied up, a hand came up from under the water and quietly undid it and pulled it out to sea. An extra person had stowed away on the ferry tonight and had snuck off before everyone boarded from the second island.

He was now climbing into the boat, taking it around the second island, where he would head for the third one. He had been there once before, you could not get past the trees near the beach, a strange gate blocked the way, and something more, it was like a dead end, it would not let you in.

Still it was a hiding place in the trees, and would do for now.

Septimus was not going to give up easily, he had been found by a large ship in the Channel. They had lowered a small boat and taken him on board, where he ended up in France in a hospital, but now, he was back. He had not understood a word said to him. In the dark of night, he had left.

Any other time he would have been noticed, but not tonight, tonight they were all 'off duty'.

A few times that evening Scarlett was aware that the Highest Order corner, as she had named it, was not quite on the same wave length and several times she caught one of the wizards or witches glancing towards her. They were all deep in conversation.

She caught a few nods of the heads or shaking in disagreement, whatever it was that was going on, one thing was for sure, it involved her and her brother.

Hey ho, no doubt they would find out soon enough. Dazlin Darren was trying to get her attention, and so was Cecily Springbocker.

Cecily handed over Scarlett the book she had requested. "Not sure why this book had been archived," Cecily explained. "Was not one that I can say I am familiar with, how clever of you to know it had even been written Scarlett."

Scarlett smiled and thanked her for it. "Surprising what you can dig up with a lot of research," she replied. If only she knew, Scarlett thought.

Darren was beckoning her over with his head, she went and sat down next to him. "Sorry, a few distractions around here tonight," she explained.

"I hope I can be another one," he smiled at her. Suddenly Scarlett felt very bashful, her cheeks reddened and she looked down towards the floor.

"Maybe you can come over to the mainland more often?" he asked her.

"I can try," she looked at him. "Or maybe you can visit here more often too?" At this point their friendship may have just taken a turn towards something a little bit more romantic.

"Dance?" he asked her.

"Don't mind if I do," she said and the pair of them found a space amongst the chaos of the evening for a little smooch.

Quietly in the corner Percy smiled at the pair, and a plan that had just been an idea in his head was fast becoming more and more part of the bigger picture, he thought.

He knocked on the table for the attention of his immortal friends and struck up a conversation with them all, Tarragon in particular.

"Thanks for getting the dish for Mason," Scarlett said. "I think he's going to be spending a lot of time messing about with that and the other equipment he wants."

"Messing about? How dare you," Darren mocked her. "It's fascinating stuff, I have something similar and I told Mason I would help him setting everything up, and get equipment for him and I to communicate with from Mainland to island too! Be glad to teach him all I know."

"Actually," Darren dug deep into his pocket, "I bought you a little something too." He gave her a small package wrapped in Christmas paper. "Not to be opened until the morning," he grinned. She gave him a little kiss on the cheek.

"Thank you," she said, now it was his turn to blush. They returned to their seats.

There was a special guest at the party now, Father Christmas himself.

A buzz of real excitement came from all the orphan children as they queued up to receive their gifts, Father Christmas did have a familiar face... looking very much like Marvello!

It really was a special night and one that would not be taking place at all if not for the actions of one special brother and sister, amongst others.

But, there was a lot more to this party than met the eye. It was a cover up really for an important meeting of The Highest Order and Percy Tatterhill, and a meeting that had just taken on a new twist, well, two of them in fact.

At the end of it all, and quite unexpected, Marvello, aka Father Christmas, gave Mason a wink as he too received a gift, as did Scarlett, Darren and Charlie. "Not to be opened until tomorrow," they were told.

All too soon it was the end of quite a fairy-tale evening and the ferry sailed away towards island two for the first drop off and then onto the mainland. Scarlett and Mason sat and watched the lit up vessel until it disappeared into the distance.

"Come on you two," their Mum and Dad were waiting to walk back to No. 1 Waters End with them.

"Have you enjoyed it?" Grace asked them. She knew she had, immensely.

"Best night ever," Mason really was buzzing, his best friend had been here a whole week, he had s.ch cool stuff already and it wasn't even Christmas morning yet. He shook the package given to him by Marvello. "Wonder what's in here?" he asked Scarlett.

Scarlett was lost in thought, so many different things running through her mind right now, and a cold shiver ran over her. "Come on, let's get back," she said.

Mason knew that he would be having a good look round when he got back in his room, Charlie wouldn't leave without doing something.

He also smiled, knowing that his friend had left with more than he came with, giant spiders that

Mason had found in the house several weeks earlier were now buried among his friend's clothes. He burst out laughing at that thought.

In the dark of the night and among the edge of the trees on island three, Septimus had settled down, and had just made himself a large bonfire. He was rubbing his hands together, it was really cold, his next job was to make himself some sort of a shelter here out of these trees.

What was that? He could hear something near him, something above his head, he looked up to see where the noise was coming from.

He squinted, it had gone quiet, imagining things, he thought, probably the fire crackling. He was wondering how he could get back onto Waters End without being seen, he had to find that hidden treasure now. He thought back to all the places he had searched already, over and over again.

Not aware, that at this moment in time $1/5^{th}$ of a huge amount of treasures was buried deep in this island, but it was not somewhere he could get to, even if he wanted to.

More movement from above, what *was* that?

Island three had some very interesting keepers, they were not as gentle as the runners that had been placed on island two, no sir.

These creatures were the Monksters, so named because they very much resembled small Marmoset monkeys in the body but by no means cute of the face. They had hideous faces, very scary looking.

A description of them would be:-

A good 12" in height
Around 15kg in weight
Arms and legs of monkeys
Colour, beige fur
Heads... awful
Eyes as big as saucers
Fangs for teeth
Bat like ears
Tongues of lizards.
Talking, no
Flying, yes.

These creatures lived just in the trees and among the steep cliffs at the back of this island which was very similar looking from the rear as island two.

In fact, island four and five were quite similar too. Island six was a large island with a difference, the difference being a small volcano right in its centre.

At this moment in time they were observing this strange person beneath them and very soon they would start their attack, which would not be nice.

They took their role as island keepers very seriously, no unwanted guests here. Mr Spangles had no need to take official reports from them nor on the remaining islands as each one housed something more and more unfriendly. He would just fly over at night to observe, that's all that was needed, but this night, he would not be.

There were two yelps in quick succession. Mason had searched his room and looked under his pillows, hmmm nothing. Pity for him he did not check at the bottom of his bed under the duvet, too late... he yelped out.

Very soon afterwards, Septimus Dread was jumped on by a dozen all biting, all scratching and kicking screaming beasts. He yelped in surprise, these things hurt. He got to his feet, running, desperately trying to get them off. They were all clinging to him.

He spun around trying to shake them off, running as quick as his feet would carry him into the water. Only then did they release their grip and stand in a line on the beach, screeching. He would not be back in a hurry.

Covered in blood and looking more threatening than ever, the big man got back into the boat using just his hands as oars, he was that desperate to get away.

Mason was chucking everything out of his bag looking for the medic kit... he would kill Charlie.

Elvira was now back inside No. 5 Waters End after a very mixed evening. Joy at being in the company of her fellow immortal friends and apprehension in finalising the plan for the next quest.

In comparison to what Scarlett and Mason had to do the first time, which could be deemed as child's play, the next quest really was grown up stuff. Each quest would get worse, and more difficult. The dangers were very real. They had no idea what was to come.

She gazed into her crystal ball and scanned the island, and also now the second island as it too now 'open' and the process of protecting it was in place.

Oh, what was this? She zoomed into the water as a small boat was racing along shooting past island two and heading for Waters End.

"Septimus," she exclaimed. "Is there no getting rid of you?" She summoned Mr Spangles, instructing him to make great haste to Dino at the Hidden Bay. They must apprehend their unwanted visitor as soon as he came ashore.

Not wanting to spoil the evening for the others before Christmas, her best bet was to alert Freddie Spinner and Basil. They would deal with this intruder.

It was quiet on Christmas Day at Waters End after all the mayhem the night before, and at the foot of Scarlett's bed was a pile of presents. She had no objection to being treated as a child one day of the year, it was rather sweet, also at the foot of her bed was Astro, curled up and snoring gently.

First of all, she was intrigued by whatever it was that Darren had given to her. She took the small package from her locker and opened it.

Inside was a dainty silver necklace with a heart shaped locket, and a note which simply said *I hope we can be more than friends*.

Whatever else she opened this morning, this would outshine them all. She was touched, and she hoped they would too, he was growing on her! She put it on.

"Wake up sleepy head," she nudged Astro, she had something special for him, his very own collar and tag, with his name and address.

Next on her opening up list was whatever it was that Marvello had given to her and Mason. She ripped it open. "What on Earth?"

Inside was a drawstring bag with a note, *'Do not pull cord'* and a set of instructions.

Only pull cord when ready to use. Fully charged for first use.

And the diagram showed a set of goggles that were rather ordinary looking. Once the cord was pulled on the side of them two things happened. A front part fell down that inserted over your nose and mouth giving you a one hour air supply, and secondly a small hose from the side that clipped to your clothing instantly making everything waterproof.

This gadget was known as the watersporter, and was solar rechargeable. Scarlett placed it into her bag. She then set to opening everything else up before leaving her bedroom.

Mason was still asleep having had to apply sting cream three times the night before.

It was a bit of a clue, Marvello's gift. The portal for their next quest would be reached not from Elvira's house at No. 5, but via the Stream in the enchanted part of the forest, where there was a deep whirlpool that would bring them directly out to the similar stream back at the cottage at Fira's Lair.

Fira's lair was no longer, but this area was still enchanted and was now home to Tarragon the Warlock, a second cottage housed Druleus. There was no longer a barrier. In its place was a preventative swamp far too wide and deep for any to try and cross, running around the middle of the forest.

The way back would simply be in reverse, but only

after full charge of the watersporters. No full charge meant no way back.

A tunnel was the only means of getting from the Cottages to Westings mainland and beyond. It ran from in between the two cottages and the other end was placed inside a small cottage, up on a cliff away from prying eyes. The cottage belonged to a lesser wizard.

The ticking tocking portal at island two which led directly to *The Realm of the clocks of time* was lifted into the air and transported onto island three, and guarded by the Monksters.

The portal from Elviras house to Westings mainland was now closed. The timeless horses were now back in *The Realm of the clocks of time*.

Christmas Dinner was a fabulous one and despite his red appearance, Mason was distracted by his pile of presents. He too had a watersporter from Marvello which was in his bag, and a whole abundance of everything space like and other worldly to distract him.

Septimus had a different day, covered in bandages having been sorted out by Basil. A bit of antiseptics and stitching up, a tetanus boost with a very large needle for good measure, and a nasty dose of medicine that was not required.

He was being detained in an empty storage facility, had been fed and watered, and suspended in mid-air by Elvira for the time being. She would call Percy.

Hanging up on a wall in his luxury Georgian house, Percy had a very large map of the islands. Waters End was always lit up around the edge, now island two had the same small lights around the edge.

The other five remained dark.

He had just taken a phone call from Elvira and instructed her what to do next. Septimus would not like this, not one little bit.

He was to be the new caretaker at *The Camp of Curious Creatures*. He would spend all his hours under the watchful eye of Dino and Freddie building many animal homes there, and keeping them all clean.

Anywhere outside of this area was totally banned to him, and this would be enforced by a tagging device permanently attached to him with an electric charge activated should he try to get out of the area. It was this way, or leave permanently.

Septimus did not want to go anywhere, still under the delusion that somehow he would find the hidden treasures. It was a plan, for the future.

The sand duners, and runners were his first arrivals to accommodate. All other care of the creatures was now allocated to Beanie.

The next morning Scarlett and Mason went to the waterfall as instructed the night before, to collect a lot more coins that were waiting there for them to transport. The coins had accumulated there over the holiday. This money was now earmarked for something else on the agenda.

Once they had loaded their bags, Mason had an idea. "Why not try out our new watersporter equipment here before we go to Elviras?"

"Why not indeed?" Scarlett agreed, she couldn't wait to try hers too. They put the goggles on and pulled the cords. Straight away, nose and mouth pieces came down and clamped onto their faces and then the small hose pipes with clips dropped down.

As soon as they attached these to their clothes it felt like a rush of warm air all over them from the top of their heads to the soles of their feet.

Scarlett dipped her leg into the water and took it out again, it was bone dry. She gave Mason the thumbs up and they both jumped into the water.

They went under and found it very easy, they were able to breathe easily. Then they found themselves being pulled downwards faster and faster until they were swirling and swirling around, it was a bit like going down a giant plug hole at great speed.

Faster and faster they went, not able to control what was happening. They were travelling at incredible speed.

Suddenly they felt themselves being pulled upward higher and higher and then their heads were above water again. They looked around, this was not the water that they had just jumped into. They swam to the side and got out.

It was familiar to them, taking off their goggles the apparatus pinged back to its original state and the energy bar at the top said 89% energy left. Well that much was okay then, but where were they?

They headed forwards and once again heard the familiar music surrounding them and realised that they must have gone back in time again, but through a different route. They had been here before, it was Fira's Lair.

In a few minutes they arrived, but now there was

not one cottage, but two. They knocked on the door and it opened up, they walked inside and there sitting at the table was Tarragon.

He looked surprised to see them, "You were not to be due here until this evening, once the new portal had been approved and checked both ends."

They seemed puzzled. "We went to get your coins and tried out some new equipment, that's all," explained Scarlett.

"Yes that's right," agreed Mason. "We just jumped in the water and then ended up here."

Tarragon looked very worried. "Come with me," he said. They followed him back to the stream.

"What you have done," he said whilst walking quickly, "is put yourselves into the next portal before being instructed to do so, it was not ready."

"How so?" asked Scarlett.

Tarragon exhaled deeply, "A portal has to be enchanted at both ends with spells and magic, you were just told to collect your coins and go to Elvira as usual."

He went on to explain that once there, Elvira would have shown them that the portal at her house was no more, it has been closed.

"And then she would have shown you the new way. It has only been partly activated her end only, once here I would have done the same and completed the return portal. Both ends should have also been protected first."

"Where is the return portal?" asked Mason.

"You mean where *was* the return portal," Tarragon pointed, "you were to go back the same way you came in the stream."

The stream was no longer there, the magic had been broken. Now what? How would they ever get home again. They had made a huge error.

The brother and sister were now stuck in The Middle Ages.

TO BE CONTINUED…

EPILOGUE

Scarlett and Mason ... In the wrong lifetime

Scarlett and Mason Beckett had just travelled through a portal in time, and they had made a big mistake. They should not be here.

Not only were they in the wrong time era, they were now stuck in The Middle Ages with no way to get back home.

All they had for company were a Warlock and a Wizard but neither had the power to help them. An unfinished spell from 600 years in the future had left them stranded.

This time they were really on their own, how on Earth could they get back to their family, they were in deep deep trouble ... the way was shut.

Printed in Great Britain
by Amazon